"Ready?" Tessa asked.

Braden nodded and gestured for her to go first. They wound through dark shadows toward the exit leading to the livestock pens. At the back door, Braden stopped Tessa. "We're good to go. No sign of Vic, though."

"He could be in the booth."

Braden searched ahead. Spotted a man on the ground, his legs poking out behind the booth.

"Man down." Adrenaline kicking in, Braden reached for Tessa to leave.

Something small suddenly came flying out of the booth. Little sparks of light lit the night. Explosions sounded. Quick, staccatos. *Pop. Pop. Pop.* Firecrackers!

The horses spooked. Thankfully, the gate was locked.

Braden took a firmer hold on Tessa and started her in the other direction. Another set of firecrackers flew into the middle of the herd. Exploded.

A horse bumped the gate. It swung open. The animals stampeded out. One after another, they barreled down the chute toward them. Toward Tessa.

Braden's gut clenched. He hadn't reacted fast enough. There was no easy escape from the crazed horses.

Susan Sleeman is a bestselling author of inspirational and clean-read romantic suspense books and mysteries. She received an RT Reviewers' Choice Best Book Award for *Thread of Suspicion*. *No Way Out* and *The Christmas Witness* were finalists for the Daphne du Maurier Award for Excellence. She's had the pleasure of living in nine states and currently lives in Oregon. To learn more about Susan, visit her website at susansleeman.com.

Books by Susan Sleeman

Love Inspired Suspense

McKade Law

Holiday Secrets
Rodeo Standoff

First Responders

Silent Night Standoff
Explosive Alliance
High-Caliber Holiday
Emergency Response
Silent Sabotage
Christmas Conspiracy

The Justice Agency

Double Exposure
Dead Wrong
No Way Out
Thread of Suspicion
Dark Tide

Visit the Author Profile page at Harlequin.com for more titles.

RODEO STANDOFF

SUSAN SLEEMAN

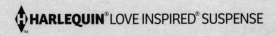

HARLEQUIN® LOVE INSPIRED® SUSPENSE

Recycling programs for this product may not exist in your area.

LOVE INSPIRED BOOKS

ISBN-13: 978-1-335-54375-2

Rodeo Standoff

Copyright © 2018 by Susan Sleeman

www.Harlequin.com

Printed in U.S.A.

And Joshua said unto them, Fear not, nor be dismayed,
be strong and of good courage.
—*Joshua* 10:25

For my family, who I often took for granted growing up.

Acknowledgments

A special thank-you to Ginger Solomon for naming Tessa's horse Copper and to Lisa Hudson for naming Braden's horse Shadow. I greatly appreciate your help!

ONE

Tessa kept her eyes trained on the deadly threat.

The eighteen-hundred-pound bucking bull's menacing glare stole her breath. She couldn't think. Act. Or move.

He tossed his head, his beady eyes immediately locking on her as if she had a bull's-eye painted on her chest. He snorted. Shifted his massive black-and-white body, ready to attack.

He was coming for her, if she didn't do something.

But what?

She'd come to the arena for some quiet time—a moment to think and prepare for the upcoming event. Instead, she found herself alone with an animal that shouldn't have even been there, and she had no experience handling a crazed bull. None!

Don't panic. Keep calm. Don't set him off.

She shot a look around the open-air rodeo arena, searching for an answer. Law enforcement had prepared her for many situations, but her deputy training never covered facing down an angry bull. Even after participating as a barrel racer in hundreds of rodeos, she knew very little about bulls, other than that they were fast when they charged. She couldn't outrun this creature to reach the safety of the spectator stands. No human could. If she was foolish enough to try, he'd ram his horns into her body before she got to the wall. And she'd never turn her back on him, anyway. No way, when his reaction time was much faster than hers.

Then what?

Please, please show me a way out of this.

She shifted her feet. Just a few inches. Felt the gun in her ankle holster that she always carried off duty.

Slowly, she bent down, her fingers creeping along her leg. She inched her pant leg up to her knee. In one swift motion, she grabbed the gun and rose.

The bull huffed and pawed. Rubbed his head in the dirt, a sign of extreme distress.

Dumb move, Tessa. Totally the wrong choice. Her sudden change in position had spooked the huge animal. Continued movement could cause him to charge. He would slam that hard head into her body. His tipped horns still deadly, he'd toss her into the air like a rag doll as she'd seen happen in countless rodeos. Cause internal bruising at the very least, organ damage likely. Death at the worst.

She lifted the gun. Aimed. Regretted having to use it, but knew she'd have to fire if it came down to her life or the bull's.

"Rrrrrumph. Rrrummph," he grumbled, then started tossing his head.

He was claiming his territory, getting angrier. His charge was imminent. She sighted the gun. Dropped her finger to the trigger.

"Hey, bull," a deep male voice called from the stands.

Tessa's gaze shot to the far end of the arena, shocked to find a cowboy climbing a gate when no one was supposed to be there. He was silhouetted against the rising sun, his hat pulled low, his shoulders broad.

The bull swung his head toward the sound. The cowboy vaulted over the railing and dropped onto the sandy rodeo soil. "No need to use your weapon on the bull. I've got this." He removed his hat and waved it at the bull. "Hey, bull, over here."

She searched his face to see if she recognized him, but he was half a football field away, and she couldn't make out his identity. She opened her mouth to call out to him. To tell him to get back in the stands, but something about his confident stride told her he knew what he was doing.

Besides, shouting would just draw the bull's gaze back to her.

The beast turned, his big lumbering body spinning faster than she would've imagined a nearly one-ton creature could move. He planted his hooves with a solid thump. She'd seen many a cowboy trampled by similar hooves and knew the severe damage they caused.

"When I get him over here," the cowboy called out, his tone calm as if on a pleasant outing instead of facing a monstrous animal, "I want you to head for the stands. Slowly, so you don't draw his attention again. Don't speak. Just give a single nod if you understand."

She tipped her head in the briefest of nods.

The bull pawed at the ground and growled, his tone low—a warning.

"Hey, bull. C'mon. Let's get you moving." Waving his arms again, the cowboy backed toward the return gate where bucking bulls and broncs exited an arena after the competition ride ended. Tessa knew from watching bull riding that breeders trained rodeo bulls on basic behavior, so the bull should recognize the gate once he got close and would know he could safely leave through it.

The bull started moving. Trotting at first. Then picking up speed, his head low and ready to connect with the man's fit body.

"Go now," the cowboy called out to her.

She backed toward the stands, keeping her eyes pinned on the grumbling animal.

One foot, then another, she told herself to keep her fear from taking hold and making her bolt for the stands.

Inch by inch, she moved, making sure she didn't add even a smidge of extra movement.

The powerful cowboy stood tall. Her rescuer. Confident. Brave. Her hero.

The bull reached full speed. Hooves thundered over the soil. Rapid. Racing.

God, please, she begged as she continued to back away. *If You're there, please keep this cowboy safe.*

Braden kept waving his arms to make himself a target. He had to. The bull could turn on a dime and still charge the woman. She was inching toward the wall just as he'd instructed. Thankfully, she didn't bolt like a frightened calf. If she did, he couldn't do anything to stop this monster from chasing her down.

Once she was safe, he fully intended to question her about her reason for being here with a bucking bull. Just as important, the law enforcement officer in him wanted to know why she was armed for a visit to a public arena.

"C'mon now!" Adrenaline he hadn't felt since

leaving professional bull riding raced through his body.

The bull charged closer, his hooves kicking up dirt.

Twenty feet. Fifteen. The urge to run grew with each step, but Braden stayed firmly planted in place to keep the bull moving forward. At the last second, he would climb the gate to get out of harm's way.

Timing was everything.

Ten feet. Five feet.

Just a little longer. Hold steady.

One second. Two. Three.

He jumped up. Clasped the steel railing. His heels hooked onto metal rails and held fast. The bull continued his course. Plowing closer. Pummeling the ground.

Five seconds to impact. Braden held his breath. The bull swerved right and charged through the return gate as his training dictated.

Braden blew out a breath. Jumped down and swung the gate closed. He secured the latch. The bull peered over his shoulder, his gaze still menacing.

"I'm not sorry to ruin your fun, fella." Braden let out another long breath, the adrenaline riding out on a wave of air.

Footsteps pounded on concrete, heading toward him. He spun. Saw the woman running along the lower-level spectator fence. How she hadn't collapsed in a puddle of relief, he had no idea. Most people would have fallen apart after narrowly escaping a run-in with a bull. But, on the other hand, most people would have had the sense to avoid that kind of showdown in the first place.

Braden crossed the grounds to give her a piece of his mind for putting herself in this situation. Lifting his hat, he swiped away perspiration with a handkerchief. Always hot in Texas in the summer, forecasters predicted this Fourth of July weekend in Lost Creek to be a scorcher, and he already missed his air-conditioned apartment in Austin.

Head down, her hat shadowing her face, the woman threw a leg over the top of the fence. He didn't want her to get hurt climbing down, so he slammed his hat back on and offered his hand.

She looked up. Fixed her gaze on him.

Tessa McKade.

He hadn't seen her since he quit riding bulls six years ago. Not even when he volunteered at the events to promote the sport of bull riding. Not surprising he hadn't run into her, he supposed. He'd mainly worked PBR—Professional Bull Rider—events dedicated solely to bull riding, and she was a barrel racer.

He reached up to lift her down by clasping his

hands on her trim waist. She smelled like apple pie and sunshine and all things American, as he'd known she would if he'd ever come close enough to engage in a conversation with her.

Just touching her caught him unaware for a moment. He thought to let go but held on long enough for her sapphire blue boots below her nicely fitting jeans to hit the dirt. "Are you okay?"

"I'm fine thanks to you." She frowned. "Well, maybe my pride is a bit damaged from needing to be rescued by the great Braden Hayes."

Surprised to hear his name, he was caught off guard. "You know who I am?"

She shoved a wispy strand of fiery-red hair up under her hat. "Everyone in the rodeo world knows a two-time PBR champion."

He tried not to frown, but he hated that people saw him only as a PBR champion, when he'd done so many important things since those days. Of course, he should've expected it when he volunteered for rodeo events and put himself back in the spotlight. He didn't much like that part of the PR gigs, but he wanted to give back to a sport that he'd once lived for. For such a cause, he would put up with the way others gushed over him.

He met her gaze. "I don't believe I've had the honor of officially meeting the great Tessa McKade. What is it, eight or nine years running as the local barrel racing champ?"

Her mouth dropped open as if she found it unbelievable that he knew her name or anything about her for that matter. But he did. Or, at least, he thought he did from watching her compete for several years before he retired. Her earnest and naive personality had been refreshing in a place where scantily dressed women threw themselves at him just because he could stay on a bull's back for eight seconds. She had been in her early twenties back then and rarely interacted with others on the rodeo circuit. Most of what he knew about her had come secondhand, or been observed from a distance. Still, something about her coffee-colored eyes that seemed to see the world in a different way had caught his notice.

She speared him with a tight gaze, but it quickly softened. "Nine years, but that's not important. I need to thank you for saving my life."

"What in the world were you doing in here with a bull, anyway?"

"It's not my fault." She lifted her chin and eyed him. "I was here first. Someone added the bull later. I didn't even know it was here until I turned to leave."

Say what? "Bulls aren't quiet creatures, so how's that even possible?"

She pointed at headphones circling her neck and turned to peer in the other direction. "I was in the middle of the arena, facing away from the gate. I left it open when I came in. No biggie as there isn't supposed to be any livestock here at this hour."

She paused and shook her head. "Anyway, I was listening to the announcers call my past rodeos. It's my pre-rodeo ritual every year. Get in here at sunrise each morning for a couple of days before livestock and participants arrive. Sit in the middle of the arena listening to the past rodeos to psyche myself up for the upcoming one."

"So who wants you dead, Tessa?"

"Dead?" Her wide-eyed gaze met his. "No one that I know of."

"Well, someone does."

Her mouth fell open, and she gaped at him. "You think someone put the bull in here to kill me?"

"Don't you?"

"Honestly, not until you mentioned it." She shot a look around the area. "I mean I haven't really had a chance to think about it. For someone to kill me, they would have to know I'd be here and I…" She clapped a hand over her mouth.

"What?" he asked.

"The local news did a story about me the other night. I mentioned this pre-rodeo ritual. Means plenty of people would know I'd be here today." She bit down on her lip for a moment. "But still, murder? That's a little far-fetched."

"C'mon, Tessa. You're not thinking straight. We're talking about a bucking bull weighing nearly a ton. Putting an animal like that in an enclosed ring with an unprepared person is tantamount to murder."

She wrung her hands together and tears looked imminent before she faced the chute where the bull was still shuffling around and huffing. A violent shudder claimed her body.

She was upset now. He suspected it was far more than the near run-in with an angry bull. His blunt talk about murder was likely the cause, but he needed to be frank to get her to realize the danger she'd been in. The danger she could still be in.

"I hate to admit it, but I guess you're right." She sighed. "Seems like someone did try to kill me, but why?"

"Since this attempt involved a bull, we could be looking at one of your competitors." He held up a hand when she looked like she planned to argue. "And before you think that's too crazy, my years as a homicide detective prove that people don't always think rationally. They commit murder for the craziest of reasons, and if they fail, they often try again until they succeed."

She looked at him then and stared, her full lips pursed. He'd had many a thought about those lips back in the day. She might have been more of a tomboy then, but her innocence had drawn him like a magnet. He'd never followed his attraction as he avoided serious relationships, and she seemed like a serious kind of woman.

She swallowed hard. "You went into law enforcement?"

"Austin PD."

She tilted her head in question. "I never pictured you as a cop."

"Never thought you pictured me at all." He grinned at her.

A flush of red surged over her face. How cute. She was still a breath of fresh air. He had to admit the fact that she'd given him more than a passing thought warmed his heart, and he widened his smile.

She ran a hand over her hair as if embarrassed and she was trying to smooth it away. Even cuter.

"Why law enforcement?" she asked.

He was enjoying the innocent flirting, but he wouldn't continue and make her more uncomfortable. "I was looking for the same adrenaline rush I got from bull riding."

"And did it pan out that way?"

Thoughts of his former partner, Paul, going off on his own while hopped up on adrenaline came to mind. Paul had lost his life that day, and Braden started questioning his reasons for being a cop. Not something Tessa needed to know about, so he simply shook his head. "But I found out I loved the job and worked my tail off to move up to homicide detective. So I know what I'm talking about when I say you're in danger. I noticed the lock to the gate was cut when I came in. Means we aren't looking for someone with a key, but can you think of anyone who might be responsible?"

"I'd hate to think one of my competitors would stoop this low just to stop me from winning again."

"Then who?"

"I don't know. Someone related to my job, maybe. I was a patrol deputy for years, and now I'm a crime scene investigator."

Explained the gun. "It's a great possibility someone you arrested or you testified against is out to get you." He made strong eye contact to drill home his next point. "Regardless of who is responsible, we need to proceed as if you're still in danger until proved otherwise."

Her gaze wandered to the bull again, and she fanned her face. "I need to call Harley and tell him what happened."

Braden knew she meant Harley Grainger, President of the Lost Creek Rodeo Association, who'd also arranged to bring Braden in for the competition to help draw a bigger crowd.

Tessa glanced at her watch and dug out her phone, then tapped the screen. "He's not due in for an hour or so. He'll want to get someone out here for the bull now, so I'm calling him. Then maybe I can figure out who the animal belongs to and how he got here, and you can be on your way."

"I'm not leaving your side," Braden said, irritated that she was so eager to get rid of him. "Not when you could still be in danger."

She shot him a look of annoyance. "Don't let my size fool you. I'm a deputy for crying out loud. I can take care of myself."

Yeah, Paul had made a similar statement, and Braden had vowed he'd never leave a person unprotected again. "It's that kind of attitude that means I'll stay right here until I'm sure you're safe."

TWO

Tessa may have met Braden today for the first time, but after just five minutes of conversation, it was clear that he thought he knew what was best for her, and he was the last guy she wanted hanging around. His actions reminded her of his pushy behavior and cocky attitude back in the day. He'd won championship after championship, and it was obvious to anyone looking that his confidence knew no bounds. He became a big rodeo celebrity, and women in every town had tried to grab his attention. She'd seen them fawn over him, and he'd done nothing to reject the attention.

Just like her former boyfriend Jason. After she'd quit traveling the rodeo circuit to focus on school, he continued touring without her and cheated on her. She'd dumped him on the spot as soon as she found out, but the pain of his betrayal still lingered. Now here she was letting Braden's rugged masculinity get to her. Letting his smile affect her. Well, no longer. *If* she ever dated again—a big *if*—she would never ever fall for a guy like Braden Hayes.

She glanced at him as he stood watching the bull. His hands were jammed into the pockets of his faded jeans. He'd pulled his hat low again, looking like a real-life cowboy. He tilted his head, his gaze filled with longing. For the sport he left behind?

Odd. He'd voluntarily retired at the height of his success, so why the melancholy?

Maybe he was thinking about his last ride, a particularly bad one. He'd gotten his glove hung up in the bull rope, and the bull had dragged him for quite some time before Braden broke free. She was amazed he'd managed to free himself. After the bull had thrown him, he'd had to get on his feet and pull his body up on the bull to relieve the pressure on the rope so he could slide his hand out. Who had the presence of mind to do that when an almost one-ton bull thrashed you around like a dog with a chew toy?

She had to admit it would be a man who was good under pressure, like he'd shown himself to be just now with this raging bull. The massive beast hadn't fazed him a bit. She found that confidence even more appealing than his looks.

He sighed, then caught her watching him and gave a brief shake of his head.

"You miss it," she said.

He nodded.

"I don't at all pretend to understand the urge to ride a bull, but I'll understand the longing for the events come Monday."

He turned eyes the color of a stormy sky on her in a pensive gaze. "How's that?"

"This is my last competition. My horse, Copper, has health issues, and it's best for him to retire."

"You could get another horse."

"No," she said firmly. "Copper loves to race, and I'd feel like I was cheating on him with another horse. And even if I didn't feel that way, when you barrel race, you're putting your complete trust in something that doesn't communicate with words. Takes a lot of training to succeed. I have far too much going on in my life to find time to train a new horse."

"At least I never had an emotional connection to a horse to worry about." He smiled.

"No, you just had to worry about keeping your body in one piece." She ran her gaze over him. He was a good four inches taller than the typical five-foot-ten professional bull rider, and he was still fit. Really fit. In spite of herself, she was attracted to him. Drawn to him. To that smile. Those compelling eyes.

He cleared his throat, and she suddenly realized she was staring at his chest. She jerked her head up to find his smile had turned flirty.

"Do you recognize the bull?" she asked, quickly returning her focus back to where it needed to be.

He let his eyes linger for a moment longer, awareness of her remaining, then shook his head. "I've been out of the business too long. Nowadays, I only know the top bucking bulls I see at the big PBR events."

"Hopefully, Harley can give us the owner's information."

"If not, the bull's ear is tagged, and we can check the RSR."

"RSR?" she asked.

"Rodeo Stock Registry of North America, a genetic DNA database that holds parentage records and tracks offspring of bucking cattle."

She gestured at the arena's main entrance. "Here comes Harley now. Let's hope he can ID the bull, and we won't have to go that route."

A dark-headed Goliath of a man dressed in jeans, boots and a big Stetson, Harley stormed across the arena carrying a white binder. He lifted his hat and swiped his arm over his forehead. "You sure you're okay, Tessa?"

"Fine, thanks to Braden."

"Harley Grainger." He planted his hat on his head and held out his free hand for Braden.

"Good to meet you in person. I'm sorry about the incident."

Braden took what looked to be a firm grip and shook Harley's hand. "Think nothing of it. I was glad to help Tessa out."

Harley swung his head to look at Tessa. "Your dad's gonna have a fit when he hears about this. I've been friends with him so long I feel like you're one of my own girls, and I let you both down."

"I saw on the way in that someone cut the lock," Braden said. "People can hardly hold you accountable for someone cutting the lock."

"And you're only responsible for livestock once they're checked in," Tessa added and squeezed Harley's arm. "You had no reason to even be here before the livestock were supposed to be delivered. I get that and Dad will, too."

"I thank you for understanding, Tessa, but you know your dad has different standards as the sheriff." He frowned.

"Are you worried about something else?" she asked.

"Attendance. Pure and simple. This crazy heat wave is already threatening to keep folks home this year, but once this story gets around town, it could give them another reason to stay away."

Tessa hadn't thought of that. "You can spin it with the press as a handsome cowboy rescuing a damsel in distress. Who knows, it might draw even more spectators in."

"You think I'm handsome, huh?" Braden whispered.

She started to roll her eyes, but his flirtatious behavior, so like Jason's, didn't even deserve that much of a response.

"I'm sure glad you agreed to come down for the rodeo," Harley said, obviously missing the undercurrent running between Braden and her. "Wish you'd told me you were arriving this early. I'da been here to greet you. Maybe then things woulda been different."

"Maybe," Braden said.

"Why *were* you here so early, anyway?" Tessa asked.

Braden turned toward her. His lazy hooded eyes ran over her and made her feel like she was the only woman on earth.

"Like you," he said, "I wanted a little time alone to relive the glory days."

"Well, it's a good thing you were here, for Tessa's sake and for our program. I'm especially grateful that you'd come an extra day before the rodeo begins, when we let our fans take a close-up look at the livestock. You usually do the bigger PBR events, so I figured you'd turn me down flat."

"I like to help out the smaller venues when my schedule allows."

Really? Sounded like he actually cared about the success of small-town rodeos. About the people and volunteers. Maybe he had layers she hadn't seen before. Still, one layer didn't make him a man she could trust.

"I hate to do this to you," Braden continued. "Especially with the issue of attendance, but I'm planning to help find the jerk who put the bull in the arena with Tessa. Means I might have to sit out a few of the PR events I agreed to handle."

Help find the suspect? That was news to Tessa. She opened her mouth to tell him that wasn't necessary, but Harley said, "That's right, you're a detective now." Harley pursed his lips for a moment. "Wish you hadn't hung up your spurs. You were something to watch."

Braden suddenly gestured at the bull as if ignoring Harley's compliment, at odds with the guy who'd seemed so cocky when he'd won so many championships.

"I'm hoping I can use my experience in the ring and as a detective to close this case," he said. "First step is to figure out who put the bull in the arena. We have a little over two days before the rodeo opens to figure that out and we shouldn't waste any time. Harley, if I give you the bull's ID number, can you give us his registration information?"

"Sure thing," Harley replied.

Braden clambered up the rails to reach for the bull's electronic identification tag fixed in his ear and called out the number. He could still move fluidly. Surprising, what with all the injuries bull riders sustained. Of course, he must have recovered from his injuries, or he wouldn't have passed a police physical. But she'd seen him take some bad falls, and a bull's jarring motion takes a toll on hips, shoulders and knees, so he had to have residual effects.

"Here it is." Harley tapped his notebook. "He's King Slammer. Belongs to Ernie Winston Bucking Bulls out of Waco. He's on the check-in schedule for nine o'clock."

"He's several hours early," Braden said. "Do you make the check-in schedules?"

"Other volunteers handle that." Harley, like everyone else in the association, was also a volunteer. Not unusual for small-town rodeos. "This year Douglas Peters is in charge of it."

"Douglas?" Tessa stiffened.

"Is he a problem?" Braden asked.

"I'm…not sure. His sister is Felicia Peters, my biggest competitor. Neither of them has made any secret about not liking me. In fact, Douglas often accuses me of cheating."

Braden's eyebrow went up, but he didn't speak.

"Everyone knows the Peters family doesn't

much like Tessa," Harley said. "But I can't imagine Douglas being behind this."

Tessa wasn't sure she'd be that generous. Douglas had been pretty nasty in his accusations against her.

"Let me give Ernie a call to see what's going on with King Slammer." Harley stepped away and lifted his phone to his ear.

Braden hopped down, standing tall and ruggedly handsome with his hands on his waist, his feet planted wide. Tessa's gaze wanted to linger, but she forced her attention to the crime scene. She walked along the outside of the chute looking for any clue that might lead her to the person who wanted to end her life, but she couldn't focus. She'd done her best to put on a good front for Braden and Harley, making it seem like the bull was no big deal. But she was smart enough to realize that someone wanted to cause her great harm, and she suspected when that someone learned she'd survived, they'd try again.

Her phone rang and she dug it out of her pocket. Her father. Great. Could she get away with ignoring the call? As the Lake County sheriff, he usually received news long before anyone else, but he couldn't have heard about the bull already, could he? She could just see him going ballistic once he did. Then, like always, he'd warn her to be careful. He told her brothers, Matt and Gavin, to get after things, but he tried to coddle her and her sister, Kendall. She loved him for his caring but was exasperated at the same time.

And she couldn't ignore his call. He could need her on an important investigation. Forcing herself to sound cheerful, she answered.

"Got a report of a stolen bull," he said before she could tell him about King Slammer. "It was taken from the rest area just outside town. We're talking a fifty-thousand-dollar animal. I need you out there ASAP to process the scene."

"A stolen bull at the rest area," she said, catching Braden's attention. "Do you have a name for the bull?"

"King Slammer."

She shot a look at the chute, her mind processing the idea that someone stole this bull to use it as a weapon against her. "No need to search for him. I'm at the arena, and you can tell the owner that King Slammer is here."

"What in the world?"

"Someone dropped him off. Not sure who yet. Harley's here now, and we're figuring it out."

"Well, I'll be." The words drew out in his deep Texan drawl. "Why steal a bull just to leave it at the arena when it was scheduled to be delivered to the pens there anyway? Truck and trailer there, too?"

"I haven't been outside since I laid eyes on

the bull, but I'll check it out before I process the scene."

"I don't much cotton to such a high-dollar theft in my county, so take your time and don't miss a thing. Matt's at the rest area and will handle things until you get there."

She was glad her brother, a county detective, caught the case instead of the other detective on staff, as Matt had a better case-closure rate.

"Go ahead and look for that truck and trailer before heading out here, too," her father added.

She was about to hang up when Braden came toe-to-toe with her and grabbed her phone. "Sheriff McKade."

She tried to retrieve her phone, but Braden spun, keeping it out of her grasp. "Looks like King Slammer was put here to injure your daughter."

"Who is this?" she heard her father demand.

Braden identified himself and added that he was a police detective in Austin. "I want to accompany her to the rest area, but law enforcement professionals often refuse to believe they need help. I thought maybe you could convince her to let me escort her." He listened carefully, then handed the phone to her. "He wants to talk to you."

She put the cell to her ear. "Dad."

"Listen, Tessa. You may be a grown woman,

but don't think that means you can purposely avoid telling me about something like this. You hear me, girl?"

"Yes, Dad." She wanted to stand up for herself, but she wouldn't engage in a personal argument with Braden standing close by. She could and did glare at him for snatching her phone, though. He simply peered at her with a blank expression as if he hadn't done anything wrong.

"Braden Hayes is going to accompany you to the rest area," her father continued. "And I'll be meeting you there, too."

"Dad, I don't need anyone to watch over—"

"Hold it right there, Peanut. You need the family's help and, right now, Braden's, too. And I want to meet the man and shake his hand. If he hadn't come along…" His voice broke.

His obvious concern for her safety put her closer to crying than anything that had happened since seeing the bull pawing at the ground right in front of her.

"I'll see you as soon as I'm done here," she managed to mutter through a throat that was closing and ended the call.

She stowed her phone and glared at Braden. "You had no right to do that."

"Easy, darlin'," he said, his words languid and low. "Or you're likely to rush off into danger, just the opposite of what your father and I want."

She couldn't handle that he'd aligned himself with her dad on this issue, but arguing with such a mule-headed man wouldn't do any good. She headed for Harley, breathing deep to ward off tears of frustration that would make her look like a frightened girl instead of a strong deputy.

Harley stared at his phone in his hand as if willing it to ring. "Call went to Ernie's voice mail. I'm hoping he'll get right back to me."

She told him about King Slammer's theft. "If Ernie's out at the rest area when I get there, I'll ask him to call you."

Harley nodded as Braden joined them.

Still upset over the way he'd butted in where he had no business going, she ignored him. "I'll take a look for the missing truck and trailer, then grab my supplies and process the crime scene before heading out."

"Crime scene?" Harley's voice squeaked high. "Now wait a minute, Tessa. There's been no crime committed here."

"Someone cut the lock at the gate and a stolen bull was left to stampede an innocent woman," Braden said, his tone deadly serious. "Where I'm from, we call that a crime."

Tessa stormed ahead of Braden. They'd been walking the blocks surrounding the arena, looking for the truck and trailer for some time now, and she didn't hide her anger very well. He'd have to be an idiot not to see she was mad at him for taking her phone to talk to her father. He shouldn't have done it, but come on. She needed someone to have her back right now, so he'd taken on that responsibility. If that meant invading her personal space and overstepping his bounds, so be it. Keeping her safe came first for him.

He planned to apologize. Just not at the moment. Now he needed to keep his eyes and ears open for any additional threats.

"Doesn't look like we're going to find the truck, so time to move on." She spun and marched back toward the arena.

They passed the barn that would soon house contestants' horses, then crossed the street to the large parking lot surrounding the building on three sides. On the backside, outdoor pens connected to gates leading to the chutes where bulls and broncs would enter the arena. A sign saying *Danger Bulls, Stay Back* hung from the fence. Tessa breezed right past it without a hitch in her step, but the irony wasn't lost on him.

She stopped at a full-size pickup and reached into the jump seat to pull out a tote bag and a case that resembled a large fishing tackle box before returning to the chute still holding King Slammer.

Braden watched her for a moment as she squatted by the cut padlock dangling from a thick chain. He enjoyed the way she attacked her job with the same intensity he felt for his work. Her gaze didn't seem to hold as many questions as it had in the past, and in the years, she seemed to have grown stronger. Even more attractive than her understated beauty.

He was drawn closer to her and would love to know more about her. For now, he'd stick with quizzing her about her job. "Do you always carry forensic items in your truck?"

"Basic stuff, yeah." She flipped open the hard-sided case. "When I'm on call, I often need to go straight to a scene and don't always have time to pick up the county vehicle."

Braden nodded. He stayed on alert, his senses attentive to any unexpected noise or flash of light, but he let his eyes follow a soaring red-tailed hawk swooping over the open-air arena built in the 1930s. The bird's terracotta-orange tail feathers glowed in the bright sun, beauty only God could create.

As a kid, Braden had often gone outside to take solace during his parents' fights, and it was part of why he loved outdoor venues. With many of the PBR events now held in large indoor arenas, small venues run by volunteers were a breath of fresh air. Literally. Still, if this had been a big venue, they would have had paid security staff, thus preventing the threat to Tessa's life.

"Which do you like best?" he asked her, wanting to hear one thing about her personal life. "Riding in an outdoor or indoor arena?"

"I grew up on outdoor ones, so that's still my preference." She snapped on latex gloves before opening the case.

"Mine, too. I love the connection to God."

Their gazes connected, a hint of respect in hers, and he felt like the simple exchange cemented something between them far bigger than their preference in arena styles. She tilted her head to look at him, a look of interest darkening her chocolate-brown eyes. As quick as the look came, it evaporated. She clearly didn't want to acknowledge her attraction. He had to admit her rejection stung. Was it because he rarely received rejections or was it because she was special?

He almost sighed, then stopped. He was letting his interest in her take over and that was a recipe for disaster. He took in a deep breath and let it out, hoping to clear his brain and move on.

Investigation. Think only investigation.

She started assembling a metal frame with a board at the base. Over the top, she placed a plastic bag.

"What's that?" He bent down to take a better look.

She scooted back as if he carried the plague. Would she be reacting this way to any man or was it him? He got the feeling that it was him, but he didn't know why.

"This is a portable fuming chamber," she said, her tone filled with enthusiasm for her work. "I'll place the lock inside the chamber with cyanoacrylate—otherwise known as superglue—and the fumes will adhere to the prints and change their composition to make them visible. I can then enhance them with powder and even photograph them."

"I don't know much about forensics, but wouldn't you find the prints by dusting the lock right from the start?"

She eyed him for a moment, her expression tightening before she jerked her gaze away to stare off into the distance. "This way is more thorough. Someone put a bull up close and personal with me. I could have died. Not something I'll ever forget, and I don't want to miss a single print."

Taking an extra step to find the person who tried to kill her was a good sign. Coupled with her earlier cautious awareness of her surroundings, he was glad to see that she wasn't as willfully blind to the danger as she'd first led him to believe.

"Plus, fuming hardens to secure the fingerprint in place and stabilizes it for transport with minimal risk of destroying the print." She poured water into a small bowl and placed it on the chamber base. She carefully removed the lock and balanced it upright next to the bowl, then ripped open a foil-lined envelope. "This is the fingerprint developer—the cyanoacrylate."

"That word rolls off your tongue like you've been doing this for some time."

"I have a Master's in Forensic Science and have been County's lead crime scene investigator for two years, so I've used the word quite a bit." She hung the envelope from the top hook.

"But you're still a deputy, right? I mean, you said you were a deputy when you told me to back off."

"I hope you didn't take any offense to that. It was just me being ornery—a knee-jerk response over the way my brothers and father try to coddle me. I don't need someone else championing the same cause." She met his gaze and held firm. "I really can take care of myself, and after you shake hands with Dad, you're free to go."

We'll see about that. "You were explaining how you're both a deputy and a crime scene investigator."

"Right." She started rolling the bag down the frame. "County requires all investigators to be sworn officers and work patrol for a minimum of three years. I always knew I wanted a forensics career, so I worked as a patrol deputy part-time while getting my degree. When I graduated, I'd fulfilled the time requirement and could move into the first investigator opening."

"Sounds like you enjoy your job."

"Enjoy…yeah, but the word doesn't do justice to the way I feel about forensics." She tucked the bag under the frame. "It's my passion."

"So is barrel racing, right?"

She frowned.

"Did I say something wrong?"

"Since I'm retiring this year, it's kind of a sore subject with me."

"Right." The urge to take her hand and offer comfort, something a deputy wouldn't appreciate at all, almost took over his common sense. Almost, but he stifled it. Still, he couldn't help but wonder about Tessa the woman, not the deputy. Would she reject his comfort? With the way she'd scooted away from him a few minutes ago, he had to think she would.

She got to her feet. "The fuming can take a few minutes. While it works, I'll search for additional evidence."

"What about the gate itself? Don't you want to check it for prints, too?"

"I will, but this is a public gate. Means there'll be tons of latent prints, and it'll take some time for our examiner to get through all of them. Of course, I'll have him start with any prints located on the lock. That will give me a place to start the investigation."

"Wait, what?" He gaped at her. "You're not going to try to handle the investigation yourself."

She eyed him over her shoulder. "Wouldn't you if you were me?"

"Yeah, but I'm a detective and you're not."

"Doesn't mean I don't know how to follow leads."

"You're too close to the situation."

"Like I'm going to let that stop me." She moved slowly down the side of the chute, stirring up King Slammer, who head-butted the rails.

Braden had to give Tessa credit, she didn't even flinch. Usually, he admired a feisty personality, but now? She didn't have the training to handle an attempted murder investigation and could get hurt along the way. In spite of that, he didn't need to protest, as he doubted her father would let her run the investigation, anyway.

She squatted and picked something up that looked like the tip of a latex glove. She stared at it, her face screwed up in earnest concentration. Her concentration was so complete that he was convinced she was oblivious to her surroundings.

Totally oblivious. If he wasn't standing watch, someone could easily attack her.

He had years of experience in catching killers and would-be killers and she needed his help.

She didn't realize it yet, but he'd make sure she figured it out. No matter what it took. He had to get through to her, before another attempt on her life caught her unaware and succeeded.

THREE

Near the arena gate, Tessa kept her focus on the shoe print created by a leaky water trough. She felt Braden's intense gaze on her. With the way she was reacting to him, maybe it should be unsettling, but with a big strapping lawman keeping an eye on her safety, she didn't have to think about protecting herself at the moment, allowing her to work faster.

Question was, why did he have such an overwhelming need to be looking out for her? Maybe it was the chemistry between them. She felt it deep in her core, and he'd made no secret that he was aware of it, too.

But that was even odder, right? She was nothing like the kind of women she'd seen him with in the past. And a handsome guy like Braden would have his choice of women. He wouldn't have to go out of his way to help her just because they were attracted to each other.

Argh. She needed to stop speculating on his

response to her. It was just a waste of time, when the last thing she needed was a man like Braden in her life.

She forced herself to concentrate on the treads embedded in the mud. She wasn't a shoe print expert, but an athletic shoe with a crack in the sole made this one stand out. Odd. Most people associated with the rodeo wore cowboy boots or Western work boots.

"What are you working on?" Braden squatted next to her.

At his nearness and the smell of his minty soap, her heart fluttered, but she ignored it. At least she tried, but she struggled not to pay attention to the way his gaze fixed on her and didn't let go.

She swallowed hard before speaking. "I'm trying to determine how fresh this shoe print might be to figure out if it's from our thief."

"How's it even possible to determine the freshness?"

"See how the water from the dripping trough is running along the gutter? Only the tip of the print's toe has filled with water, indicating it hasn't been here long. If it had, the rest of the print would be flooded."

"Looks like an athletic shoe, but that's an odd type of shoe to wear for someone who'd steal a bull, right?"

"Right. Which is why I was debating if it's important." She stood to put some distance between them. "I'll cast it just in case."

He came to his feet and remained standing far too close for her liking. "Anything I can do to help?"

Move away so those startling blue eyes don't distract me. "You can mix the powder while I take pictures. I'll be right back with the items."

Feeling like a coward racing away, she hurried to her truck to grab a zipper bag of dental stone and pour the correct quantity of water into the bag. She took a few deep breaths for good measure, then returned.

She handed the bag to him. "Simply mix this with your hands, making sure to get into all the corners so we use all the dental stone."

"Maybe I should close the bag so I don't risk making a mess."

She shook her head. "Closing it could cause pressure and the bag might rupture."

He started mixing, and she laid an L-square near the print to demonstrate the size of the shoe and started snapping pictures.

"If I had to guess, we're looking at a male's size ten shoe," Tessa said.

"A pretty common size."

She nodded and confirmed she'd taken clear photographs, before putting the scale back in her tote and holding out her hand. "I'm ready for the bag."

He set it on her palm. She took the top of the bag in her other hand and was careful not to touch him. She squished the liquid, about the thickness of pancake batter, to make sure Braden had thoroughly mixed all the lumps. Satisfied, she poured the casting material, moving over the length of the indentation and extending out a few inches until she'd covered the entire print.

"How long will this take to dry?" he asked.

She looked up at him. "I would have thought a detective might know some of this stuff."

He hooked his thumbs in the corner of his belt loops near a large PBR championship buckle. "I suppose I should at least have a passing knowledge, but I figure that's why we have forensic professionals on staff, and I leave it to them."

She'd heard that plenty of times from deputies—including her family. "From my point of view, it's always helpful when the detective at least knows how long things take, so they don't nag me for results."

"I guess I'm guilty of that, too." His lips tipped up in a playful smile that she'd seen him flash at the press and at fans plenty of times in the past, and even knowing it meant nothing, maybe less than nothing, her heart flip-flopped.

"I think I'm going to learn a lot being with you," he said.

"About that." She stuffed the empty bag into her tote and leveled out her tone to keep her wayward emotions out of her voice. "Let me give you a pass again on this babysitting detail. Dad will expect you to come along and shake his hand when I go to the rest area, but then you can get on with your weekend."

"I'm good with sticking around." His tone was causal, but irritation flared in his eyes. "You didn't say. How long for the cast to finish?"

Good. Keep the focus on the investigation. "With this weather, I'd say twenty minutes and it'll be set for transport."

"And then what?"

"Then the cast sits in the lab to cure for seventy-two hours before I can wash off the dirt and clean it for analysis."

A thick eyebrow arched. "That long?"

"It has to fully cure, or I could compromise the details of the casting."

He kept watching her, his gaze warm and familiar as if they'd known each other for years. She had a bizarre urge to run her finger down a long scar on his cheek that a bull had likely inflicted. Instead, she smoothed out the liquid so once it dried she could write the forensic collection details on the back of the cast.

She wished he'd walk away, but she supposed it was her fault that he remained so close. She'd all but taunted him into learning about her job, and now she would have to pay the price of his nearness.

Braden shook his head in disbelief. His first day in Lost Creek wasn't even over, and he was approaching the second crime scene of the day. Craziness. He was on vacation with a little PR volunteering thrown in. Just a few days to attend the rodeo to help friends and enjoy time away from the rigors of being a homicide detective. But this? Tessa. The stolen bull. Not at all what he had expected.

She parked close to the yellow crime scene tape cordoning off the rustic rest area. A tall male deputy stood just inside the perimeter talking to another man who was clenching and releasing his hands. Braden figured he was King Slammer's truck driver.

"My dad isn't here yet. Something must have come up." Tessa shifted to peer at Braden, fatigue dawning as if she was coming down from the adrenaline. "I suppose since you took my phone and proved how pushy you can be, it's too much to hope you'll wait in the truck for my dad to arrive."

"Sorry about grabbing the phone," he said sincerely. "I just didn't think it was a good idea if you took off on your own, and I knew I didn't stand a chance of convincing you on my own. Plus, I can help you here. I'm a detective, after all."

She pointed at the men. "So is my brother Matt."

"But is he a bull expert? Because if he is, I've never seen him at a competition. I can tell you if any evidence you collect regarding the bull is off. Can he?"

"Fine," she said reluctantly. "You can come with me. Just don't get in the way." She hopped down and grabbed her equipment from the jump seat. She stacked several cases under her arm and looked like the weight or bulk, or both, might take her down.

He tried to take the largest case from her.

"Look." She stepped back. "I don't want to come across as ungrateful for your rescue—and for your ongoing offer of help. I am and will always be most grateful to you. I owe you my life." Her tight rein on her emotions seemed to be failing, and she bit down on her lip as if she didn't want to lose control.

"It's okay to let go, you know," he said. "Anyone who's been through what you've experienced today would be shaken up."

She took in a long breath and shifted her cases. "I'm good."

She was simply acting as any law enforcement officer would in this situation, and he didn't take it personally. "I always knew you were gutsy."

"Always?" She eyed him, her gaze digging deep. "We just met."

"I watched you compete plenty of times." *And watched you off your horse, too.*

Her eyebrow went up, but before she could comment, her brother slipped under the fluttering yellow tape and jogged toward them, taking her attention. Tall, powerfully built, the guy didn't look at Braden at all, and his concern tightened features closely resembling Tessa's. She frowned as he kept coming.

Matt took the equipment cases from her, and she didn't argue. He set them on the ground and pulled her into a tight hug. "Dad told me what happened. You could have been killed."

"Don't overreact. I'm fine." She struggled to get free, but Matt held on.

Interesting. Braden didn't expect her to put up the same stubborn front with her brother, but after the way she'd reacted to her father's call, maybe he shouldn't have been surprised. She acted like she had something to prove, even with her own family.

Matt let her go. "You're not as tough as you always try to pretend."

She sighed and glanced at Braden. "It's not the

easiest being the baby in a family of law enforcement officers."

"So that explains your prickly barbs," Braden said before thinking.

"Prickly?" Matt's gaze traveled between them. "She's usually pretty easygoing unless you try to get overprotective with her."

"Guess that's where I went wrong." Braden looked at her brother and offered his hand. "Braden Hayes."

"I'm Matt McKade." He smiled as they shook hands. "Come to think of it, she's the only sibling with red hair, and we used to tease her as a kid that she was adopted. She *was* pretty prickly about that, too."

"I don't need to stand here and be picked on when I have a job to do." She scooped up her cases and marched off, but Braden saw a hint of a smile as she moved away.

Oddly enough, it pleased him to see she had a sense of humor and that she could take a little teasing—at least from someone she trusted. But he wasn't here to decide if he liked her or her sense of humor.

"Mind if I hang around?" he asked Matt. "I'm a homicide detective with the Austin PD and a former bull rider. I might be able to help."

"Fine by me," Matt replied. "Not sure what

Dad will say when he gets here about how long you can stay, though."

If their family was anything like Braden's, he had no desire to get involved in their family dynamics. He couldn't even begin to imagine what it was like to work on a law enforcement team with your siblings and father. An only child, Braden could hardly stand to be in a room with his parents, never mind working with either of them. Not with the way they bickered and snapped at each other so often that they ended up ignoring him unless they needed something from him. He'd grown up with broken promises and their many failed marriages, and he still had issues trusting people, much less counting on them to have his back. The only person he'd ever really trusted was his partner on the police force, and even then he'd had reservations.

He followed Matt to the crime scene under the shade of a majestic bald cypress. Getting out of the blazing sun that had dried up most of the Texas Hill Country this past month was a welcome relief. Tessa set down her cases by the curb, then came over to join them.

"This is King Slammer's truck driver, Wyatt Adams." Matt introduced Tessa and Braden.

"*The* Braden Hayes?" Adams's eyes widened. "Man, you're like a legend. No one's managed to ride Fearless Whizz since you retired. That last time sure was something."

Braden cringed inside at the mention of his successful last ride. Successful at least in terms of the timer. But then he'd gotten his hand hung up in the bull rope, and once freed, he had been hurled to the ground and stomped on, resulting in a lacerated liver and broken ribs. "God was watching out for me."

Adams shook his head. "No sirree. Your skill got you through. You were one of the best. How come you quit?"

"I think Braden would appreciate it if we stuck to the theft," Matt said as if reading Braden's mind. "Go ahead and tell them what you told me."

Adams's eyes narrowed, emphasizing deep wrinkles in his leathery skin. "Not much to tell. Pulled in here to use the facilities and take a quick catnap. When I came out, the truck and trailer were gone."

"Did you leave the truck running?" Braden asked.

"Yeah, but I locked it. Carry an extra key just so I can." Adams lifted his chin. "Diesels are hard on starters and batteries. Leaving it running means I have to crank it over one less time, extending the battery and starter."

"Or did you just want the AC running to keep the truck cool for your nap?" Braden asked.

A sheepish look crossed Adams's face. "That, too."

Diesel truckers commonly let their vehicles idle, but if Adams had taken the keys, he wouldn't have been in this situation unless someone hotwired the vehicle, and Braden was having a hard time believing he'd risk the loss of an expensive bull for a more comfortable nap. "You're in town awful early for a nine o'clock check-in."

Adams's brow furrowed. "Which is why I was going to rest a spell."

"I get that, but why leave Waco so early in the first place when you could have slept in instead?"

"To beat traffic."

Traffic between Lost Creek and Waco on weekday mornings was rarely heavy, but Braden didn't have facts to dispute Adams's statement, so he let it go. "Who all knew when you were leaving town?"

"Let's see…" Adams paused, eyes raised to the tree, as if this was a difficult question. "King Slammer's owner, Ernie, of course. His ranch foreman and the ranch hand who helped me load the bull."

Matt fixed his gaze on Adams. "Remember, I want Ernie to confirm the names and contact information you gave me before you leave here."

Adams nodded.

"Do you work for Ernie or are you an independent hauler?" Tessa asked.

"Ernie only contracts out transport when he has several bulls signed up for the bigger rodeos. I work for him and handle his small loads."

Even more reason why he shouldn't have risked leaving an expensive bull unattended with the truck running. Braden assumed the guy would lose his job for doing so. "Have you noticed anyone unusual hanging around the ranch?"

Adams shook his head.

"How about on the road behind you on your drive?" Braden asked as he spotted a county sheriff's SUV pulling into the lot. In law enforcement, supervisors often used SUVs to carry additional gear patrol officers might need, so Braden suspected this was Sheriff McKade's vehicle.

"I don't have a habit of watching the rearview all the time. King's pretty expensive cargo, so I keep my focus ahead." Adams removed his hat and ran a hand over a bald head slick with sweat. "Man, Ernie's gonna kill me if that bull is hurt in any way."

"Trust me," Tessa said. "He's just fine and ready to rumble."

A curious look crossed Adams's face. "You the one he wanted to meet up close and personal?"

She nodded.

Adams's expression turned to relief. "He's a real ornery fella, so I'm glad you two didn't actually meet."

The sheriff exited his car and took everyone's attention as he came to full height and paused to survey the area. He was fit and over six feet tall in his navy blue uniform. He locked gazes with Braden. His piercing brown eyes gave Braden a moment of uncertainty. He doubted criminals fared well under the man's attention. He marched across the asphalt, his gaze lighting on his daughter and unfettered concern replaced the intensity.

The only concern Braden ever received from his dad was back in Braden's bull riding days. His dad constantly worried that Braden would quit earning big bucks and his dad wouldn't be able to mooch off him any longer. Braden was bad at saying no, but he couldn't stomach paying for his dad's lifestyle. That was one of the factors in his leaving bull riding at the pinnacle of his success.

He watched to see if the sheriff would hug Tessa as Matt had done, but he simply stopped in front of her.

"You're sure you weren't harmed?" He might not have hugged her, but his voice hitched and it was clear that the man loved his daughter.

"Not a scratch on me." Her lighthearted tone didn't match the rigid set to her shoulders.

He gave a firm nod and ran his fingers over a

graying mustache. Braden saw him clamp down on his jaw and work the muscles hard before speaking again. "Be that as it may, you're not to step foot out of the house without another deputy at your side until we find the jerk who tried to kill you."

She looked like she wanted to argue, but her father spun to face Adams, who stood gawking at them. "How about taking a seat on the bench over there while we have a chat?"

Adams nodded and seemed glad to escape the group of lawmen.

Walt shot out a hand to Braden. "You must be Braden. Walt McKade."

"Nice to meet you, Sheriff."

"It's Walt." He released Braden's hand. "Thank you for all you did in keeping my little Peanut safe."

"Dad, please." Tessa planted her hands on her hips. "Enough with the Peanut thing when I'm working."

Braden started to smile, but when she caught his gaze with a feisty one of her own, he controlled it. "I'm glad I was there at the right time."

Walt faced his son. "Bring me up to speed on what the driver had to say."

Matt filled him in, his narration concise and organized, impressing Braden.

"Now the question is, is this a onetime attempt to hurt Tessa or an ongoing threat?" Matt asked.

The sheriff frowned. "We have to proceed as if the suspect plans to make another attempt."

Braden nodded. "Something that could happen at the rodeo, though at this point we can't confirm that this attack is related to her competition."

Tessa planted her hands on her hips. "Don't even suggest that I bow out of the competition. We have two days before that's a factor, and I hope we have this resolved before then."

"I hope that happens, but we need to plan how we'll keep you safe in case it isn't." Walt frowned, his mustache drooping, as he looked at Braden. "I'd demand that she drop out, but she's a McKade through and through and telling her to give up on something she's passionate about would be like trying to talk sense into one of those bulls you used to ride. Besides, she'll only be in the arena for what? Fifteen seconds? Minimal exposure. Only a gun could take her out that quickly, and we've never allowed them in the arena. We search all backpacks and anyone looking suspicious."

"I don't think he's going to try anything in a crowd, anyway," Matt said. "Or even use a gun."

"How's that?" Braden asked.

"He could have shot her today, right? Instead, a bull was his weapon of choice—even though that must have taken a lot of time and planning. Maybe there's a message there. Maybe not. But either way, he acted at a time when no one was around. Used a weapon that couldn't easily be traced back to him. Says to me he's being extra careful not to get caught."

"Good point," Walt said. "And if he tries something in a crowd of witnesses, he has to know we'll arrest him on the spot, making it even less likely that he'll act during the rodeo."

"Not that you're asking me." Tessa's arms relaxed. "But I can skip the opening night ceremonies and the contestant introductions before the competition begins, too, to limit my visibility just in case. And I promise, if at any point we think fans are in danger, I'll bow out of the competition."

"You still need protection." Braden shifted his gaze to Walt. "And I'd like to help out with that going forward."

"Agreed on the need for protection, but what are you proposing?" the sheriff asked.

"As Matt said, since this attempt was made at the arena, we can't rule out a connection to the rodeo. My experience in this area makes me better able to recognize anything out of the ordinary there."

"Good point." Her father appraised him. "But why would you want to give up your free time?"

Though this had a lot to do with promises he'd made to himself after Paul died, Braden wasn't going to mention that. However, he could offer another explanation that was equally valid. "You ever have something happen on patrol where you just can't let it go? You can't put a finger on why, but it haunts you and you know you have to keep after it and see things through to the end?"

The sheriff nodded and so did Matt. Tessa even looked like she agreed.

"Well, that's how I feel. Like I have to be here to help Tessa, and if I leave, I'll regret it for the rest of my life."

An obvious look of approval crossed the sheriff's face. "Then I'm happy for your help, son. What with the Fourth of July celebration and rodeo, my department is stretched to the limit as it is. You might be a real blessing, and I'd appreciate your help this weekend."

"Hold on." Tessa held up her hands. "I can't believe you'd let a man we know nothing about into our lives like this. That you'd leave me alone with him while you go about your business."

"Seriously, girl." Her father frowned. "You know better than that. Why do you think I'm so late? I was checking him out. His lieutenant says his skills are top-notch, and he'd trust him to protect his own family, which is all I need to know. And as to our family? You know we're not going anywhere. We'll still be involved in protecting you and in tracking down this guy who wants to hurt you, but Braden here has insider knowledge we don't have and can recognize suspicious situations we'd have no idea to look out for."

"Maybe this is just a random theft." Tessa sounded like she was grasping at straws to keep from having him around and it stung. "A guy sees the truck running and decides to steal it. Then he finds the bull in the back and dumps him at the arena to get rid of him. Doesn't even look inside to see if anyone is around."

"Only one problem with that theory," Walt said, his gaze going to Tessa. "The truck and trailer were just found abandoned on the far side of town. The thief was after the bull, not the vehicle. Which is positive proof that the primary goal was to harm you."

FOUR

Silence settled over everyone and fear radiated from Tessa's gaze. Despite her obvious dislike for him, Braden couldn't stand to see her in such pain. He had to do something. Maybe if he got them talking again, it would give her something concrete to focus on and distract her from her fear.

"Can you make a list of competitors besides Felicia Peters who might want to harm you?" Braden asked her, making sure she understood it was a request, not a demand.

Her gaze shifted to him. Her fear was still rampant, but he could see her thinking over the question, mentally running through the names. "I doubt anyone would go to the extreme of killing me to keep me from winning. There has to be another reason."

Braden wasn't so sure. "I've seen murder committed for lesser reasons."

"He's right." Walt blew out a shaky breath. "We need that list."

"I'll make it when I get back to the lab."

Braden had expected her to argue, and he'd rather that had happened than seeing her look defeated.

"What about someone you arrested?" Matt asked. "They might want to get even."

"I guess," Tessa replied. "Though I haven't arrested anyone for years."

Braden thought this was a good possibility. "If they ended up doing time, they could've recently gotten out of prison with a plan to pay you back."

"I'll be glad to pull files for suspects who might pose a threat," Matt offered.

"Thanks, Matt." Tessa gave her brother a tight smile. "I really need to work this scene and get the truck and trailer processed, too. Maybe then we'll have something concrete to go on instead of standing here speculating."

Walt trained a penetrating look on her. "Don't get so bogged down in the forensics that you don't pay attention to what's happening around you. Okay, Peanut?"

"Yes, Dad." Frustration lingered in her tone.

Braden liked the sheriff's nickname for her, but he could see where it would get annoying when used on the job.

Walt swept her into his arms and held on tight,

then kissed her cheek. She shot a look at Braden, and a blush stole up her neck and face. How adorable was her continued innocence, especially in a world that had lost so much of that very thing? It drew Braden to her like a beacon in a storm.

Walt spun to face Braden and stuck out his hand. "I appreciate your help, young man, but don't you dare disappoint me."

Braden firmly met his gaze. "You can count on me."

"Walk me to the car, Matt." The sheriff didn't wait for a response but spun and headed for his vehicle.

Tessa returned to her cases at the curb where Adams had parked the truck before it had been stolen. Braden remained in place and alternated his attention between watching her and the surroundings. Evidence bag in hand, she squatted to take a soil sample. Why, Braden had no idea. In fact, he'd expected there wouldn't be much to collect here and they would have left to process the truck and trailer by now, but she was meticulous and thorough in her work. He admired her tenacity, but without any task of his own to keep him focused, it wasn't much fun standing there. He sure wouldn't have minded if the barest of breezes would pick up and send a wave of cooling air across the parking lot, as even in the shade of the tree, the afternoon sun was beating down on him. He took off his hat and fanned his face.

She glanced up at him, held his gaze long enough to fire off all his senses, then quickly jerked her attention back to her work.

What was that look all about? Had she felt him watching her? Felt his interest?

He'd have to be blind not to see she was attracted to him. He wasn't unfortunate-looking and women often displayed their interest as she'd been doing. What he didn't receive from them was the horror that followed in Tessa's eyes as if the very thought of being attracted to him made her sick.

For his part, he'd never had such a deep response to a woman. When Tessa fixed that soft gaze on him, all other thoughts evaporated. So many women had thrown themselves at him over the years. And sure, he'd gone out with a few, but he'd never connected with any of them, and eventually he'd stopped trying. They reminded him too much of the promiscuous women his father dated for them to ever win his respect, much less anything more.

Thankfully, except on weekends like this one, running into such women ended after he quit bull riding. Since then, he'd dated, but he'd been very careful to tell the women right up front that he wasn't ever going to commit to a long-term relationship. If a woman forgot his terms, and he caught even a whiff of her getting serious, he broke things off.

Another reason to avoid any emotions Tessa evoked. It was obvious that she was a long-term-commitment kind of woman. He'd give his all to protect her, but it was hands-off in the relationship department.

Remember that.

Her brother sauntered across the lot to Braden, standing next to him for some time before speaking.

"You're interested in my sister," he said plainly.

Braden had to work hard to keep his mouth from falling open. "How do you figure?"

"You're not the only detective who can read body language, you know."

Braden opened his mouth to explain that he did not intend to pursue Tessa, but Matt held up his hand. "She's a grown woman, and I'm not here to warn you off. In fact, it's about time she started dating again."

"Again?" Braden shouldn't ask for more details, but the need to know overpowered his good sense.

"Bad breakup. But that's something for her to tell you about if she decides to do so. I just want to be sure that you can keep your eyes off her long enough to notice any danger she might be in."

The comment so shocked Braden that he could only sputter in response.

"Know that the family will keep you in our sights, and if you fail her in any way, and I mean *any* way, we'll be asking you to take a hike."

Braden got the message loud and clear. "Your family doesn't beat around the bush, do they?"

"We're straight shooters." Matt planted his hand on his sidearm.

Braden swallowed hard. "So now you're saying you'll shoot me if I fail?"

"Nah. Only if you break her heart. That's a shooting offense in our family." Matt chuckled and strode off, his laughter ringing through the air.

Braden could only stand and gape after him. That was the last conversation he'd expected to have today. He glanced at Tessa to see if she'd noticed.

She was busy gathering up her equipment but soon approached him. "Did Matt say something wrong?"

Braden wasn't about to share the conversation. "Nothing I can't handle."

She quirked up a brow. He ignored it and didn't elaborate. He expected her to quiz him, but she didn't ask any additional questions.

"Time to get going." She marched toward her truck and stowed her equipment before they both climbed in. They soon arrived back in town, and she pulled up to a street corner where yellow tape cordoned off a truck and trailer.

A female deputy stood talking to a tall male. She was long and lean with brown hair pulled back in a bun. The guy was big and muscle-bound and had dark almost black hair. As if on a synchronized team, they turned to peer at the truck, and Braden took a good look at their faces. Their hair color differed from Tessa's, but he instantly marked them as McKades and groaned.

"What?" Tessa faced him.

He gestured at the couple. "How many law enforcement McKades are there?"

"My sister, Kendall, is the last of the county employees. Well, if you don't count several of our cousins." She grinned at him, and her impish look made him smile in spite of himself. "And that's my oldest brother, Gavin, with Kendall. He recently moved back to the area to get married, and he's a Texas Ranger."

What would it be like, to have that kind of family legacy? To be surrounded from birth onward by people committed to public service and protection, people you could respect and admire? Braden couldn't even imagine it.

Tessa got out and grabbed her equipment. He

joined her, and as much as he didn't like seeing her haul her many cases, he didn't offer to help again, already knowing she'd just turn him down. They strode toward her siblings, and with each footstep, he felt them appraising him.

"Squirt," Gavin said, and Tessa grimaced. "What's this I hear about you getting into some trouble?"

"*Some* trouble?" Braden said, drawing the guy's pointed study. "She was nearly taken out by a one-ton bull, and it wasn't an accident lest she try to tell you it was."

Gavin faced Braden, and the intensity on his face exceeded his father's pointed looks. "And you are?"

"Braden Hayes," Tessa tossed out as she made her way to the back of the trailer, where she set down her equipment.

"And according to Matt, the hero of the day." Kendall stuck out her hand and smiled. "I'm Kendall, and this crabby guy is our brother Gavin."

Braden shook her hand, then Gavin's, and he felt as if he was looking at Matt's twin.

"Thanks, man." Gavin released his hand and ran it over his jaw. "We all appreciate you entertaining that bull so Tessa could escape."

"Hey." Tessa pointed at a spot on the truck door. "Did y'all see this?"

The three of them moved closer, and Braden

spotted a tiny piece of pink leather caught on a jagged rivet.

Kendall bent closer. "What's it from, do you think?"

Gavin peered over her shoulder. "I'd say a glove."

"Could be." Braden took his turn studying the scrap. "But the leather doesn't look heavy enough for a work glove. If we're looking for someone connected to bull riding, I'd say it could also be part of a bull rope pad or even a protective vest that riders wear."

"Exactly why do they wear those, anyway?" Kendall asked.

"To absorb shock and dissipate the blow to the body. Also protects from punctures from a bull's horns or feet."

"So you've got a guy in this crazy tough sport," Gavin said. "And he wears pink? Who'd do that?"

"Not me, that's for sure." Braden chuckled. "In all seriousness, the vest would probably be black with a pink accent. Still, not many men would wear that, so it would most likely have to be custom-made."

"That's good, then, right?" Kendall said. "It'll narrow down the potential list of people to question."

Braden nodded. "And now that I think about it,

if the guy is worried about unloading a dangerous bull, he might put on his vest for protection."

Tessa's eyes narrowed. "I don't remember seeing anyone in a pink vest around here, but I'll ask
Harley about any locals who might wear one."

"It could also be unrelated to the theft and
someone at Ernie Winston Bucking Bulls wears
pink," Braden added.

"I'll have Matt follow up with Ernie to see
if the scrap came from one of his employees."
Tessa stared at the leather. "I can see how someone could snag a vest, but the padding on a bull
rope? How would that happen?"

"The rider could be carrying the rope over his
shoulder. Though, honestly, I doubt he'd have it
in the trailer."

"If the leather *is* from a bull rider—" Gavin
turned toward Tessa "—we've got to find this
guy and find him fast before he tries to pull anything else."

Kendall frowned and put a protective arm
around her sister. "We're taking over your care
and you're coming with us now. We won't let
anything bad happen to you, sis."

Braden didn't like the thought that she would
be out of his sight. He opened his mouth to protest, but his earlier conversation with Matt came
to mind and Braden snapped his mouth shut. He
had to heed Matt's warning and tamp down his

crazy emotions and urges when it came to Tessa. A night away from her was just what he needed.

Then tomorrow, he could concentrate on his mission and make sure he wasn't careless with her life.

FIVE

Eleven o'clock in the morning and the temperatures had already hit ninety degrees. Braden had his truck's air-conditioning cranked at maximum blast. The heat didn't seem to bother Tessa as she rode with him toward Serenity Ranch. She'd said very little since he'd picked her up at the sheriff's office, and the tension in the truck was as thick as the outside humidity.

He glanced at her as she stared out the window. She was most likely thinking about their mission. Interview Cliff Falby, the bull rider and pink vest wearer who Harley had identified. Braden turned into Serenity Ranch's drive. Crispy brown grass surrounded a single-story building that had seen better days. A large sign with the ranch's name burned into the wood hung out front of the office, where he parked.

He settled his hat on his head. "This place looks nothing like the name."

"The owner's a no-nonsense kind of guy who

says he doesn't need a pretty property to raise beef cattle. Plus, not everyone has someone like my grandmother to sew fancy curtains and keep flowerpots filled." Tessa grinned.

He much preferred this lighter Tessa to the fearful one yesterday, but he had no idea why she'd changed. He just knew now wasn't the time to be lighthearted. "Let's check in the office to see if they know where we can find Falby. And keep your eyes open."

Her smile fell, and he felt bad for spoiling her mood, but protecting her was his first priority. He slid out of the truck and hurried around to her side, keeping his gaze roaming over the area as he moved. The place looked deserted, which was odd for a working ranch.

He escorted her to the tired-looking building, staying close by in case of attack. Stacks of paper and worn ranch equipment cluttered the small space. A woman Braden put to be in her fifties with limp gray hair sat behind an equally messy desk.

"Wynona," Tessa greeted.

The woman looked up, her eyes weary, her skin weatherworn and her expression suspicious. "What brings you out here, Tessa?"

"I was hoping to talk to Cliff Falby."

Her brow arched. "Since you're in uniform, he must be in some kind of trouble?"

Tessa shook her head. "I just need to ask him some questions."

The woman glanced at Braden, and a sudden smile slid across cracked lips as she held out her hand to him. "Wynona Sanders."

He shook her hand and offered his public-appearance smile. "Ma'am."

"I'm not so old that I need a ma'am." She chuckled. "It's Wynona. I sure did enjoy watching you on those crazy bulls."

"Falby?" Tessa asked, sounding irritated.

"It's his day off, so you'll likely find him sleeping off a binger in the bunkhouse."

"Mind if we go talk to him?" Tessa asked.

"No, but I gotta warn you, he's a mean fella when he's woken up with a hangover. I oughta know. It's market day, and we needed all the help we could get to deliver cattle, so I foolishly went to ask him to work some overtime. He just cursed me out and rolled over." She peered at Braden. "But your backup looks like he can put Cliff in line if he acts out."

Braden felt certain Tessa had been a fine patrol deputy and could handle a belligerent suspect without his help, but he didn't bother saying so. "How do we get to the bunkhouse?"

Wynona provided directions, and they headed back outside.

Tessa started down a gravel path and glanced

up at him. "Don't you get tired of the way people fawn over you?"

"Wynona, you mean?"

She nodded.

"It gets old, but I'll never let on to them. People who recognize me are people who spend their money at rodeos, and they basically paid my salary for many years and gave me a nice nest egg. Plus, they're just good folk. So I try to be obliging."

She went silent for a long moment, then met his gaze, hers unreadable. "You're a lot different than I first thought."

Interesting. "Is that a good thing?"

She nodded but didn't elaborate. He wanted her to explain. To tell him what she'd once thought of him, and what she thought of him now. But he wouldn't take them into the personal realm when they were out in the open and exposed. Besides, they had a job to do here, and no time to waste. Who knew when the next attack might come?

They followed the path down to a large barn crying out for a fresh coat of paint. The whole place was in serious need of repair, and he was surprised the owners were letting it go to ruin. "No frills" was one thing—he wouldn't judge a place for not having fancy curtains—but this indicated serious neglect.

"Does Wynona own the ranch?" he asked.

"She's in charge, but her dad owns it. As his only child, I assume she'll inherit it when he passes on."

"She already looks tired of running the place."

By the double barn door, she met his gaze. "Owning a ranch is hard work. I've seen it first-hand, and I'm glad we decided to get out of the cattle business a long time ago and switch to a dude ranch. You don't have to worry about the fluctuating price of beef or feed or even think about diseases. Just give the city folks what they expect for a Wild West kind of holiday and they're fine."

"I'd fall under city folks who have no idea what ranching is really all about." He chuckled as he imagined some of the city folks he knew at the McKades' dude ranch. "I've always lived in the city."

"No…wait…" Her steps faltered. "But you're a bull rider. I figured you grew up on a ranch."

"Sorry to disappoint," he said. "I'm a city boy all the way."

She tilted her head. "So how did you get into bull riding?"

"A high school buddy owned a ranch near Austin." He started them moving again as he didn't like standing still and making Tessa an easier target. "Hal was into bull riding, so I tried it. Turned out I was a natural. His dad sponsored both of us until we were eighteen. Then I turned pro, and Hal bowed out."

"And here I thought I knew something about you. Surprises me. Among other things."

"Things like what?" he asked, as he had a burning need to know.

"Like how committed you are to finding this guy and to keeping me safe." She shook her head. "I thought you were this shallow cowboy who lived for fame and fortune, but it's looking like I'm wrong."

He laughed. "Guess I made a good first impression, then."

"No, wait, I meant it as a compliment."

"Then I'll take it that way." He tried to sound casual, but his heart swelled with the thought that now that she'd spent a little time with him, she caught hints of the man he tried to be and hadn't seemed to buy into that superficial image that most people saw. And more important, she hadn't liked that other guy. The one everyone usually wanted to be friends with. She liked him for him. Something he hadn't known very often since fans cast him into the spotlight after he'd won his first championship.

At the corner of the barn, he held up his hand. "Let me take a look first."

He half expected her to argue, but she didn't. He stepped out to see a group of small outbuildings and a long, low structure with a bunkhouse sign out front. The log building had been white-washed at some point but had faded to a dingy gray. Peeling green paint covered part of the door, the wood raw and exposed elsewhere.

"Everything okay?" she asked.

"More run-down buildings, but looks fine to me." He gestured for her to join him, and they strode to the bunkhouse in silence.

Tessa pounded on the aged wood and paint flaked off, but no one answered.

"Cliff Falby," she shouted. "Deputy McKade here."

She tapped her foot as she waited for him to answer. Braden took a moment to appreciate the way she looked in uniform. She'd proved her ability to take charge yesterday, but in uniform, she seemed even more in control. He liked that about her. Liked that she seemed to know herself. Know her purpose and where she was going in the world.

She lifted a fist and pounded harder. Kept it up until a man—Falby he assumed, as Wynona said he was the only one around—jerked open the door.

"What?" he snapped and rubbed his eyes.

Dressed only in torn jeans and a stained T-shirt, his bloodshot eyes and the smell of alcohol radiating from him confirmed Wynona's guess about sleeping off a night of binge drinking.

"Mind if we come in? We have a few questions for you." Tessa flashed her credentials.

Wariness usurped his anger, and he lifted his arm to block the doorway. "'Bout what?"

"I hear you're a bull rider now and have a few questions for you about that."

Braden didn't know how she did it, but Tessa managed to sound impressed with the guy and acted like he would be helping them out—a move that seemed to pierce straight through the distrust he'd shown from the start. Though, he still didn't act all that interested in talking.

"I'm sure you can find other people with more knowledge than me," he said through a yawn.

"Harley Grainger specifically sent me to you."

"He did, did he?" Falby puffed up his chest, and Braden knew Tessa had scored on gaining them entry.

Falby moved back, and they stepped inside the narrow building lined with bunk beds. The place smelled like bacon, likely coming from dirty dishes in the small kitchen that filled the back wall. But what drew Braden's attention was the small dining table in the living area. A bolt cutter lay in full view and a box of latex gloves sat next to it.

Braden could see how the bolt cutter would be

a common ranching implement, but latex gloves? That, he doubted came into regular use. Tessa gave him a pointed look, and he responded with a quick nod.

"You never said who your sidekick is." Falby cast a suspicious look Braden's way.

He held out his hand. "Detective Braden Hayes. Austin PD."

"Braden Hayes! I knew you seemed familiar. Watched you on TV back in the day."

Braden didn't want to give Falby time to realize that with Braden around, they had no need to ask him bull riding questions, so he said, "I'm holding a clinic for new riders tomorrow. Maybe you'd like to gear up and join me to help give out some pointers."

"Sure, yeah, if you think I can help."

Braden nodded and gave him the details on the time of the event. He really hoped Falby would show up, as Braden wanted to get a look at Falby's vest to see if it had a tear or if he'd gotten it repaired. Falby shifted his gaze to Tessa, who was crossing the room to the table.

She tapped the box of gloves. "Since when do you use latex gloves in ranching?"

"I didn't say I did."

"But they're with your bolt cutters."

"Who says those are my cutters? The other guys drop things here all the time on their way in."

"So the gloves aren't yours?"

"Never said they were."

"Mind if I take one?"

He finally seemed to come awake, and he glared at her. "Yeah, I mind."

"But why?"

"'Cause they don't belong to me." A smirk followed. "You here to talk bull riding or gloves? If it's the gloves, then I've got nothing to say to you."

His testy reaction put Braden on alert, but the fact of the matter was, this guy could be using cutters and the gloves to commit burglary. His wariness to share info about the gloves with a deputy might be because of some other crime— one not related to the attack against Tessa at all. Braden made a mental note to check with Matt to see if they'd had any unsolved burglaries in the area and pass this information on to him.

"Tell me about your bull riding vest," Tessa said.

"Now, wait a minute." Falby's radar seemed to kick in fully. "I thought you was wanting to talk about bull riding in general. But your question sounds like you're looking at me for something."

"Just wanting to know about your vest."

"No. That ain't what you're doing at all. You want to convict me of some made-up crime, and I won't give you the ammunition. Seen that happen with my buddies and look where that got 'em. A stint behind bars." He crossed his arms and cocked his head, anger building in his gaze. "You cops think all us guys who travel around the country working here and there, not staying in one place, are trouble, but we ain't."

Braden waited for Tessa to use her skills to calm Falby down, but instead of easing the tension, she glared back at the guy, and Braden could almost see steam coming out her ears. He cleared his throat to get her attention and try to tell her to cool it so they could still salvage this interview, but she ignored him and stepped closer to Falby, pulling out her phone.

"Is this you?" She opened a picture she'd found earlier of Falby riding a bull, his black-and-pink vest obvious.

Falby kept glaring at her and didn't even glance at the picture. Braden wanted to step forward and force him to look, but he held his position and let Tessa proceed at her own pace.

She shoved her phone toward Falby until he had no choice but to slap it down or take it. He grabbed it and looked at the picture.

"Not saying a word." He shook the phone, acting like it was a hot branding iron and he wanted to get rid of it.

Tessa quickly took it back. "Thanks for nothing, Falby."

She stormed out of the bunkhouse, and Braden was totally confused. She'd proved her abilities when she'd convinced Falby to let them in, then in a flash, she lost her cool over nothing, and they hadn't learned anything to help with the investigation.

He caught up to her and spun her around. "What was up with that? We needed that guy to cooperate and you blew it. If we talk to him again, I'm taking lead on questioning."

Tessa grinned at him. "Glad to hear I'm such a good actor."

"I don't understand."

She took an evidence bag from her pocket and dropped the phone inside. "I wanted Falby to think I'd lost my cool, so he wouldn't take the time to think. Otherwise, he might have refused to accept the phone when I shoved it at him."

"Ah," he said, his respect for her skills growing. "You wanted his fingerprints."

"Bingo." A self-satisfied smile crossed her mouth, and Braden had to admit, she'd done her job and then some.

Tessa settled at the work counter in County's forensic lab. Her fellow crime scene investigator Natalie Elmer sat at her workstation on the far side of the room, while Braden leaned against the wall nearby, talking to Matt on his cell phone.

Braden had called her brother to report Falby's bolt cutters and gloves. She was supposed to be developing Falby's prints on her phone, but she found herself staring ahead and thinking about how Braden kept surprising her.

She didn't want to like him. Didn't want to respect him. It was much easier to ignore his charm when she thought there wasn't anything deeper to his personality. But as they'd had a quick lunch, he'd shown her hints of his character that continued to prove there was more to him than she expected and that attracted her even more. How far might her thoughts travel if they spent more time together?

"Are you going to work on the phone?" His voice came from behind and she jumped.

She wasn't about to share her musings, so she snapped on a pair of latex gloves and fished the phone out of the bag to set it on the countertop. She tipped a jar of dusting powder over a piece of white paper and poured out just a bit before dabbing a brush in it.

"Why not just dip the brush into the container?" Braden asked.

"You don't need much powder when developing prints and this helps prevent overloading the brush." She shook the brush over the paper to eliminate the excess, then twirled it lightly over her phone, revealing several prints.

"Since they don't all match," he said. "I have to assume one set is yours."

"Yes, but I have to lift them both for a complete evidence report." She pulled out a strip of one-inch tape and pressed it over one print, then placed the tape on a fingerprint card and flipped it over. She noted the investigation, time, date and the location where she'd located the prints.

She repeated the process for both sides of her phone, developing print after print. Satisfied she'd lifted clear prints for Falby, she sat back to discover Braden was still watching over her shoulder. This closeness couldn't go on. She needed her personal space, and she swiveled to tell him so.

She looked up at him. His gaze captured hers, the feelings she'd been fighting rising to the surface, and she froze. Time ticked by. Slow. Fast. She didn't know. She was lost in his eyes. He suddenly reached up to lift a wayward strand of her hair that had come loose from her ponytail and gently tucked it behind her ear.

She snapped from her fog and lurched back, knocking over the powder and making a mess of her counter. "You startled me."

"Sorry," he said, but his perceptive look said he knew full well why she was flustered.

"I… I…need to finish the evidence log," she stammered and felt like a middle school girl with her first crush.

"Right." He took a step back. "Don't let me get in your way."

Grrr! He knew he'd gotten in her way and why it bothered her. She had half a mind to call him on it. But honestly, that look between them left her feeling raw and exposed, and she had to clear her head before she said something she regretted.

She hurried across the room to the evidence locker where she'd drop off the items she'd found yesterday. She'd been too tired from her ordeal to process it all, so she'd stowed it in the locker and had started on it this morning before Braden came to pick her up after his PR gig at the arena.

She carried the evidence bags to the counter. "I'll be working on this log all afternoon. If you want to take off, I can catch a ride home with someone else."

"I'll wait." He pulled his phone from his pocket, then dropped into a nearby chair.

She started sorting the evidence into three piles—items to log in and put back in the secured locker as it needed no processing, fingerprint cards for the examiner and the fingerprints she'd fumed from the lock. She got right to work completing the detailed log and lost track of time. When she finished, she got up to stretch.

Braden suddenly appeared to lean on the counter next to her. Other than a few times when they'd grabbed some drinks or used the restroom, he hadn't bothered her at all while she'd worked, for which she was thankful.

"So what's next?" he asked.

"I still have to run the fumed prints and process the glove, then take all the prints to our examiner. And I'd also like to head over to the arena to get elimination prints from Harley and anyone else with keys to the main gate."

"Ever thought he might be involved?" Braden asked.

"Harley?" She looked at him then. "No. No way. As he said, he and my dad are best friends. He'd never do anything to hurt me, and he has no motive. In fact, this would be more likely to hurt the rodeo attendance rather than help it, and he lives to see it succeed."

"Did you make the list of suspects Matt asked for?"

She shook her head. She'd meant to do it, but even as a deputy, it was hard to comprehend someone wanting to kill her. Sure, she'd seen criminals angry with her and her family members in the past, but if anyone had ever threatened their lives, they'd never shared it with her.

He kept watching her but didn't chastise her for not following through.

"I'll do it tonight." She gathered the items to put in the secured locker and stood.

Braden moved out of the way. "Will Harley be at the arena this late?"

"Late?" she asked and shot a look at the clock that read nearly six o'clock—an hour or so later than she'd thought. "Harley's usually there late the night before the rodeo opens, so I should have enough time to finish up here and still catch him. If not, we can go to his house."

Braden nodded his agreement, and his stomach grumbled.

"Sorry for ignoring you all afternoon. We can grab something to eat on the way to the arena. Or I can ask someone else to pick me up and you can head home."

"I'm good," he said.

She liked his easygoing personality while in the lab. She assumed this was what he was normally like when not in a dangerous situation. Jason had been high intensity and needed to be on the go all the time, whereas she liked to take lone walks and horse rides just to absorb the still of the ranch and eliminate any stress from her day.

She picked up the evidence to return it to the locker. When the items she wasn't using were stowed, she dropped into her chair and grabbed the first card holding a print lifted from the lock.

Braden leaned against the counter next to her again. He crossed his ankles in a lazy pose, looking like a contented cowboy. She could imagine him at Trails End at the end of a long day, joining her at the corral to go for a ride. And it was precisely those thoughts that were dangerous.

She clicked open the mass spectrometer software on her computer, typed in needed information and inserted the fingerprint card into the spectrometer. She kept her gaze on the computer screen until the results popped up. "Our first suspect is male."

"That black box can tell the sex?" Braden asked.

"That black box is a mass spectrometer, and it can extract amino acids from the fumed prints." She inserted the second card into the machine. "Female prints contain twice the amino acids of male prints. So by analyzing these levels, we can determine sex much faster and cheaper than having DNA run."

"Why have I never heard of this?"

"The method is new and not widely used, but I know the researchers who are working on the project, and they've shared the process with me." She sighed in satisfaction for a job well done.

"You're like a little kid in a candy store. You really do like your work, don't you?"

She looked at him to assess his reaction. "You sound surprised."

"I am, I guess. And impressed at how dedicated you are—and how completely you can concentrate on your tasks, even when you're stuck here at your desk. I don't much like being cooped up inside."

"I prefer to work alone." She quickly turned her attention back to the computer in hopes he'd leave this topic behind, as she sure wasn't going to start talking about being a loner. She ran the other prints. "The other two are males, as well."

"With very few female professional bull riders, that's not surprising. Even if we're looking for a barrel racer, she would likely have gotten someone with experience handling bulls to steal King Slammer for her."

"Agreed." She quickly moved on to the glove. She turned it inside out and removed a short length of PVC pipe from a drawer. She affixed the glove to the tip of the pipe, then after peeling off a sheet of acetate from a rubber gelatin lifter, she rolled the latex along the length of the pad.

Braden bent closer and squinted at the pad. She had the urge to touch the wavy line in his hair left from his hat. To maybe run her fingers in it to straighten it out. How could this guy mess with her mind like this?

He lifted his head, not having a clue how he was affecting her. "Are there any prints? Did it work?"

She snapped free of her wayward thoughts to tape the pad in the corners of a small box.

"We can't tell without an alternative light source." She shone a white light on the pad and pointed at a long row of prints. "Voilà. Latent prints. I'll just take a few pictures of them. Then we can deliver them along with the other print cards to our examiner, and hopefully we'll locate a match for our suspect."

SIX

By the time Braden pulled into the arena parking space, the sun was making a mad dash toward the horizon. They'd grabbed dinner at a Mexican stand and quickly devoured it in his truck, but each moment spent in the small space made something clear to Braden. They had to talk about the attraction between them before it distracted them and left Tessa wide-open to an attack.

She reached for the door handle, but Braden leaned over to stop her.

"Hey." She shot him a look. "What gives?"

"Before we go in, we need to clear the air between us."

"Clear the air? I don't—"

"Don't pretend that you haven't noticed this crazy attraction between us."

"But—"

He flashed up his hand, preempting her. "You're a sharp person, and you can't possibly be blind to it. You simply want to ignore or maybe refuse to believe we're attracted to each other. But we've got something going on here and admitting it is the first step in figuring out how to deal with things and move on."

She sighed and arched a brow. "Okay, fine. You want me to say it. I do find you attractive, but it doesn't matter. I'm not going to pursue it. Not ever."

He hated the way she spit it out like she considered him some sort of nasty disease. "Don't worry. I don't want a relationship with anyone— not now or ever. So you're perfectly safe with me."

"Good. I feel the same way."

"Because of your recent breakup, I suppose."

Her eyes widened. "And just how do you know about that?"

"Matt mentioned it yesterday."

"My brother told you about Jason?" She clamped her mouth closed, and he heard her teeth grinding.

"He didn't share details. Not even the guy's name. Just that you had a bad breakup and Matt thought it was time for you to start dating again."

"Ugh." She crossed her arms and slid down in the seat. "My brother has a big mouth."

"He cares about you and wants you to be safe and happy."

"It's still my private business, not something to broadcast to a complete stranger."

"I won't mention it to anyone else, but I do have to ask if this Jason guy might be the one who put the bull in the arena."

"Jason?" Her forehead furrowed. "No. No way. He may have cheated on me, but he's not a killer."

Ah, a cheater. The worst kind of low when it came to romantic partners. Maybe the kind of guy who would put the bull in the arena as a sick joke and not realize she might be killed. "I still think we need to get an alibi from him for yesterday morning."

"It's likely he's not even in town. Nowadays, he participates in Cowboy Christmas events in July."

"Cowboy Christmas, huh?" Braden said, the words taking him back to his early years in the rodeo and the weeks surrounding the Fourth of July when cowboys competed in as many different events as they could schedule. Each contestant had the opportunity to earn payouts of tens or even hundreds of thousands of dollars in a short time and improve their rodeo standings.

"We'll need to confirm that," he said.

She nodded, then met his gaze firmly and held it. "So is the air clear enough for you now?"

"Depends." He grinned to lighten the mood. "Will my charm and devastatingly handsome looks continue to distract you?"

She rolled her eyes and got out, but not before he caught a hint of a smile that foolishly warmed his heart. Maybe she wasn't so opposed to him, but opposed to getting romantically involved in general. She'd said she liked to work solo. Maybe since the breakup with Jason, she preferred being alone. He often felt the same way. It was easier than trying to figure out if he could let his guard down and trust other people.

They started for the arena, now quiet and dark, and he remained alert for any threat. Stock contractors had dropped off bulls and broncs, filling the pens to capacity. He noted a woman manning the main gate but also noticed a side gate not secured at all. Harley was going to hear about that.

Tessa suddenly came to a stop and gestured at a muscular guy with a black beard and matching bushy eyebrows exiting the main gate and heading their way. He reminded Braden of a lumberjack.

"That's Douglas Peters," she said.

When Douglas caught sight of Tessa, his lip curled in a sneer, which quickly gave way to a phony smile. Braden took an instant dislike to the guy and moved closer to Tessa. She cast him a suspicious look, but he remained at her side.

"Heard you had a run-in with King Slammer yesterday." Douglas's smile morphed into a smirk.

"You wouldn't happen to know anything about that, would you?" Braden asked.

Douglas turned his attention to Braden. "Well, if it isn't the big PBR star Braden Hayes."

"Harley said you made the check-in schedules," Braden said, ignoring the sarcastic bent to Douglas's tone. "Anything unusual with King Slammer?"

One of his fuzzy caterpillar eyebrows rose. "You getting involved in this?"

Tessa pulled back her shoulders. "Braden's a detective with the Austin PD, and he's helping Matt find the culprit."

If Braden didn't know better from her ongoing frustrations with him, he'd think he detected admiration in her tone.

"Then I'm obliged to answer your questions, I suppose." Douglas didn't look too happy about it. "The schedule was pretty straightforward. Had to make a few changes to accommodate some of the owners. Par for the course, but there was nothing odd about King Slammer."

"You're sure?" Braden gave the guy his best interrogative stare.

Douglas met it without a hitch. "Positive."

Braden handed his business card to the guy. "Call me if you think of anything that might help."

"Will do." He tipped his hat at Tessa, revealing a gleaming bald head. "Best wishes on the competition, Tessa."

She nodded, but as Douglas stepped away, Braden heard her say, "Right." And he had to agree with her assessment. This man didn't wish her well, and that put him at the top of Braden's suspect list right alongside Falby.

Tessa marched toward the entrance without a backward glance to see if Braden was keeping up. He was beginning to realize she had the fiery personality associated with redheads. "Take a few deep breaths to clear your head so you don't make a costly mistake," he warned her as he kept pace at her side.

Surprisingly, she listened to him, slowed her walk and took breaths in sync with her steps. They reached the main entrance, where an older woman in jeans, a plaid shirt and a white cowboy hat manned the gate. She set down the clipboard and smiled at Tessa, then looked at Braden.

"Nana, this is Braden Hayes," Tessa said.

The woman, who he put to be in her seventies, grabbed Braden's hand and shook it as if she was pumping water from a well. "Betty McKade. I will forever be in your debt, young man. Anything you need while you're in town, just ask."

"Thank you, but—"

"Do you like blueberry pie?" She continued to hold his hand.

"Yes, ma'am."

"I happen to be famous for them. After I heard about your rescue, I made one for you."

He eased his hand out of her tight grasp. "That wasn't necessary."

"Don't bother arguing with my nana." Humor glinted in Tessa's eyes. "I get my stubborn streak from her."

"That she does." The older woman smiled, and Braden saw the strong resemblance to Tessa. He suspected she would be just as beautiful in her older years—something he wouldn't mind seeing.

Seriously? Where'd that come from?

"We should get going," he said to cover up his gaping stare.

"I'm shocked that no one has invited you for dinner over at our ranch. Not last night or to-night." Betty eyed Tessa.

Tessa sighed. "And by someone, she means me."

"So I shouldn't tell her dinner tonight consisted of a quick burrito in the truck on the way over here?"

"Tessa McKade, I declare," Betty scolded. "You sure don't know how to treat the man who saved your life."

"Yeah, you could have at least bought me a taco, too." He grinned at her, but she didn't respond with anything more than a glare.

Betty laughed. "You come on by the ranch for pie with the family when you finish for the night. I know everyone wants to properly thank you."

"Yes, ma'am," he said, as he suspected she wouldn't take no for an answer.

"Handsome and polite." She thumped Tessa's arm.

"What was that for?" Tessa asked.

"Just wanted to make sure you recognized it." She chuckled.

Braden wanted to laugh, but at Tessa's frustrated look, he stifled it.

"I assume Harley is still here," Tessa said.

Her grandmother nodded. "All the volunteers except your granddad have signed out. I was just going to lock the gate and bring Harley the sign-in sheets, so I'll walk with you."

Braden thought Tessa might march ahead as she was all-fired eager to resolve this investigation, but she waited for her grandmother to secure the turnstile and lead the way.

Inside, Braden searched sections of the arena where the lights had been turned out and cloaked the area in darkness, looking for any threats. He spotted an older man, his eyes narrowed, swiftly heading in their direction.

"Hold up," he said to Tessa. "Guy approaching at a clipped speed."

"Nothing to worry about." Betty glanced over

her shoulder at Braden. "That's my husband, Jed. His intensity comes from his many years as Lake County sheriff. He'll be tickled to hear that you considered him a threat."

Braden looked at Tessa. "You didn't mention him when we were talking about law enforcement officers in your family."

She arched a brow. "I can list the retired folks if you want me to, but it'll take a while. There's been a McKade as sheriff and/or deputy since the 1800s."

"Point taken." Braden finished his sweep of the area. He found nothing amiss, but something made him uneasy, and he didn't let his guard down.

They found Harley standing outside the press box. Tessa's grandfather had just joined him. They surveyed the arena, a proud look on their faces.

Tessa stepped up to her grandfather. "Great job on hanging banners this year, Granddad."

His stooped shoulders rose. "Some years we get the right number of advertisers for perfect symmetry."

"Granddad, this is Braden Hayes," Tessa said.

"Jed McKade." He offered his hand to Braden. "Thank you for saving our Tessa."

"Glad to help." Braden shook hands and was

impressed that the older gentleman still had such a firm grip.

Her granddad slung an arm around Tessa's shoulders and knuckled her head. "Now, you be careful, you hear?"

"Always. Braden and I'll be over for dessert soon. I've been told it's blueberry pie, and maybe Nana will let you have ice cream, too." She reached up on tiptoes and kissed his wrinkled cheek.

A stab of jealousy bit into Braden. Not only for the sweet kiss she'd bestowed on her granddad's cheek, but for her family's obvious display of affection with one another. He'd never known such love. Would never know it from his parents. Or even his grandparents, who he'd only ever met twice in his life. But as a kid, this was how he'd imagined a loving family would act. He'd given up on a dream family eons ago and now had no need in his life for family anymore. He was doing fine on his own.

So explain the longing in your heart.

He nearly groaned over the way his thoughts kept wandering to areas he didn't often think about. But then, he pretty much only hung with guys at work and didn't often see such displays of warmth, so the thoughts never surfaced in his usual routine.

Betty handed her clipboard to Harley. "I was

just about to turn this in when Tessa and Braden arrived to talk to you."

"You're here to see me?" Harley frowned. "Please don't tell me you have bad news."

"No bad news. I just need to get your fingerprints."

"Mine?" Harley's voice shot up.

"Relax. You're not a suspect, but your prints are likely on the cut padlock, and we need to be able to eliminate them."

"Oh, right." He sighed. "What do you need me to do?"

Jed's eyes lit up. "She's going to use that new handheld fingerprint scanner."

Tessa removed the scanner from a box, confirming her granddad's statement, and she looked about as giddy as he did.

"I know you want to see it in action, Jed." Betty linked her arm in Jed's. "But we need to get going."

She started them moving. Jed glanced back, his desire to stay obvious. Braden couldn't imagine what it would be like to retire from his law enforcement job. He needed it. Like breathing. Serving the public as a police officer meant everything to him, and he'd have to be forced out of the job. Just like he'd have to be forced away from protecting Tessa. Until they closed this case, he would put his all into that.

"Harley, you have an unsecured gate." Braden described the location. "I'm not sure your security procedures for—"

"That was Douglas's responsibility tonight." Harley took off his hat and slammed it against his thigh. "He said he was checking them before he headed out. Must've missed that one."

Missed it on purpose, Braden thought but didn't share. If Douglas was behind the bull attack, he could have seen them sitting in the truck, then pretended to leave and planned to sneak back into the arena to try to hurt Tessa again. She cast a knowing look at Braden, and her eyes narrowed as she swept her gaze over the empty arena.

She tried to hide it, but he could see that she was afraid. Made Braden's gut hurt. Also made him want to protect her even more. He ran his gaze over the place, not liking the way shadows had deepened with the sun's disappearance.

Volunteer or not, Harley had to do a better job on security. "Can we count on you to make sure the gates are secured at all times?"

"I'll need to push the volunteers to work longer hours." Harley frowned. "But we've got some great people here in Lost Creek, and once they hear about the problem, they'll step up."

Braden nodded his thanks but decided he'd continue to monitor the gates himself, and he'd ask Walt to get his deputies to check on them during their routine patrols. There was no such thing as too secure.

Tessa typed on the scanner's small keyboard, then held it out to Harley. "Press your index finger in the slot."

Harley, lips pursed, complied. "Never thought I'd see the day when I was treated like a common criminal."

"Now, Harley." Tessa peered at the reader, likely verifying it had captured a clear print. "You know that's not what I'm doing."

"I know, it's just this all has thrown me for a loop. Guess our little town isn't like it used to be."

Crime had invaded every inch of society, but still, this idyllic community had fewer deadly crimes than Austin. Living in Lost Creek would be a nice change from the horrors Braden saw on a daily basis.

Tessa carefully recorded the next print. "I'll also need the names of anyone else with a key to the lock so I can record their prints, too."

"Yancy Tate, Perry Richter and Vic Johnson have keys," Harley replied. "Yancy and Perry have gone home, but Vic was working bronc check-in today, and I haven't gotten his report, so he's probably still out at the pens."

"Perfect," Tessa said. "We'll head out there before we leave. Can you call Yancy and Perry and ask them to come down to the sheriff's department for printing? The sooner, the better."

"Sure," he replied but didn't sound enthusiastic. "Would be good if you could get this all buttoned up soon."

"We're doing our very best."

"Sorry." Harley sighed. "I know you are, sweetheart. I just have to be patient. But you know how I love this rodeo and want it to succeed. Not just for me, but for all the volunteers. And for the local business owners depending on attendance."

Tessa patted Harley's shoulder. "Everything will be okay, Harley."

He cast her a skeptical look.

She started packing up her kit. "It will. Just have faith."

Braden almost snorted at her comment. Faith was easy to talk about, but so hard to put into practice. At least for him. Sure, he was a man of God, but his childhood left him wary of trusting others. Who knows, maybe that meant he didn't rightly trust God, either. If he did, he might be able to see God's plan in the attack on Tessa, but Braden couldn't see an upside to it. Not at all.

"Ready?" Tessa asked.

Braden nodded and gestured for her to go first. They wound through dark shadows toward the exit leading to the livestock pens. At the back door, Braden stopped Tessa before she marched out into the open. "Let me take a look outside."

She seemed like she wanted to roll those chestnut eyes again, but she nodded instead. In the crisp night air, he searched the length of the property. Livestock rutting around in their pens was the only movement he spotted. He didn't see this Vic Johnson guy, but a small booth sat by the livestock sign-in area. Braden suspected it had been constructed to keep the volunteer cool in the heat of the day, and that was most likely where they'd find Vic if he was still there. If not, then the volunteer in charge of livestock security for the night would likely occupy it.

Braden curled a finger at Tessa. "We're good to go. No sign of Vic, though."

She joined him. "He could be in the booth."

He pointed at the arena wall. "Take the inside."

"Please."

"Please take the inside." He added a smile but didn't receive one in return.

They followed the wall for a good distance, and at the chutes that let livestock into the arena, they crossed a driveway to the actual pens. Tessa was now out in the open and the building no longer protected her. Braden didn't like it. Didn't like it one bit. If Tessa was concerned, she didn't show it. She entered the main chute to the pens like she owned the place and headed for the booth.

Braden searched ahead. Spotted a man on the ground, his legs poking out behind the booth.

"Man down." Adrenaline kicking in, Braden reached for Tessa to move her to safety.

Something small suddenly came flying out of the booth. Little sparks of light lit the night. Explosions sounded. Quick staccatos. *Pop. Pop. Pop.* Firecrackers!

The horses spooked. Thankfully, the gate was locked.

Braden took a firmer hold on Tessa and started pulling her in the other direction. Another set of firecrackers flew into the middle of the herd. Exploded.

A horse bumped the gate. It swung open. The animals stampeded out. One after another, they barreled down the chute toward them. Toward Tessa.

There was no easy escape from the crazed horses. Braden's gut clenched. He hadn't reacted fast enough. And now they were going to die.

SEVEN

Frenzied horses. Galloping. Charging. Dirt flying. Dust clouds suffocating.

Tessa froze in place. Not for long. Just a moment before she came to her senses. She turned to flee. Heard the broncs coming closer.

She couldn't outrun them. No way.

She had to go up and over. She jumped up on the rail. Her boot slipped off the metal. Caught in a lower bar, tangling her leg. She struggled to get it free. Couldn't.

"No!" she cried out.

Help us, Father, please.

"Hold tight." Braden quickly freed her leg and tossed her over his shoulder in one swift move. He climbed the rails so quickly it was as if her weight made no difference. The horses raced past. One of them caught Braden's leg.

He wobbled. She flailed out her hands to try to balance them, but he pitched backward over the rail and into an open field. He landed on his free shoulder, coming to a rest on his side. The impact jarred her teeth and stunned her brain. How must it have affected him? Seeming unflustered, he maneuvered around until he completely covered her body. Their eyes met. His were wide with alarm, as he seemed to hover over her and time stood still. She heard the thunderous horse hooves as they stampeded on the other side of the rail and was so thankful for Braden's quick thinking.

He suddenly shook his head. "We can't stay out here in the open."

Before she could respond, he was up—lifting her to her feet with one hand and drawing his sidearm with the other. "Stay by my side. It'll keep you safe if someone fires from the booth."

Braden took off, and she had to run to keep up with his long strides. When she fell behind, he scooped her up with his free arm and pressed her against his side, then picked up the pace. He barreled across the road toward the grandstand, where he slipped underneath the structure and lowered her to the ground behind a girder that hid her from view. She peeked out to see the horses fleeing the pen, running in the opposite direction from where she and Braden had hunkered down, clouds of dust trailing them.

"Vic!" Tessa said in a sudden moment of realization. "It had to be him by the booth. If he's unconscious, then he can't do anything to protect himself. Someone has to help him."

"There's nothing we can do for him now without risking your life."

"I have to go to him."

"No." Braden took her arm and held firm. "This isn't about Vic. It's about you, and you have to stay here to prevent another attack."

She met his gaze. Felt his strength. Still wanted to go, but nodded her agreement.

"Call 911." Braden turned to watch over the road. "And stay behind the girder."

She moved back and dug out her phone. Her hand shook as she punched in the numbers.

"911. What's your emergency?" Tessa recognized the voice as belonging to dispatcher Odessa Killeen.

Tessa described the incident but didn't mention it could be a second potential attack on her life. She requested two units. One deputy to file a report of the incident. The other to check on Vic. Or maybe it wasn't Vic who they'd seen— it could be whoever was in charge of keeping an eye on the pens that night.

"Matt and Seth are both about three minutes out." Odessa referred to Tessa's older cousin. "Let me get them dispatched."

"Tell them Detective Braden Hayes is with me, and he's armed."

"10–4." Silence fell over the conversation, but Odessa soon came back. "They're both on their way. Matt will check on the injured man. Seth will take your statement. And assuming this guy has taken off, I've put out an alert for a suspicious male fleeing from the area."

"Perfect. Thanks." Tessa hung up and called Harley to let him know about the horses so he could round them up. She took a deep breath and blew it out to release her adrenaline before dialing her father and recounting the incident.

"And you're okay?" His worried tone raised her unease.

"Yes, thanks to Braden." She stared at the back of Braden's bare head. He must have lost his Stetson in the field. She owed him so much. If not for his fast thinking when he freed her trapped leg, the broncs might have trampled her to death.

She could still hear the pummeling hooves and could almost feel the solid horseflesh taking her down and the hooves connecting as they raced over her body. A shudder raked through her and tears started to form.

"Where are you now?" Her father's insistent voice broke through her thoughts. She searched deep for the control she'd learned to possess as a deputy to force away her tears and gave him her location.

"I'm on my way," he said, and she didn't even

attempt to tell him to stay away. She knew he had to see for himself that she'd come to no harm and nothing she could say would stop that. She ended the call, her tears still threatening.

Father, please help me keep my cool. No one needs to see how rattled I am.

She stowed her phone, and once she regained her composure, she relayed the plan to Braden.

He glanced back at her. "You think Vic set off the firecrackers?"

"Vic? No. I can hardly see why he'd want to hurt me. But he'll need to be questioned."

"If it's not him, the suspect was either hanging out here, hoping you'd come back, or followed us from the lab."

"I hate the thought of this creep tailing me, but it's a good possibility." She curled her fingers and let the nails bite into her palms. The small pain let her focus and helped to keep her fear at bay. "There has to be other explanations, too."

"What about Douglas?" Braden asked. "He left the gate open. He could've snuck back in, overheard us talking and knew we'd be coming out here."

She let his statement ruminate for a moment. "No one could've known in advance that I would be here. So it has to be a crime of opportunity. Means Douglas wouldn't have any reason to be carrying firecrackers."

"With it being the Fourth, lots of people have fireworks including illegal ones like firecrackers. He could have firecrackers in his vehicle, and when he heard you were going to the pens, he seized the moment."

Tessa nodded, as it was a logical explanation. "I'm sure Matt will search his truck, but if Douglas has half a brain, he'll get rid of any firecrackers he might still have."

The wail of two sirens spiraled through the air, and Tessa soon heard a patrol car screech to a stop nearby. Braden stowed his weapon, and she stepped out from behind the girder in time to see Seth climb from the vehicle. He was tall and muscular with blond hair cut short on the sides. There were no horses in sight, but Matt arrived from the opposite direction and parked by the pens, where he would check on Vic.

Seth acknowledged Braden's presence with a quick nod but trained his steely blue eyes on Tessa. "Tell me what's going on."

She shared the incident again. Matt's voice came over Seth's radio, telling him that it was indeed Vic on the ground. Someone had hit him from behind, then gagged and tied him up, but he was okay.

Thank You, Father, for protecting him.

"You think this was another attempt on your life?" Seth asked.

"Yes," Braden replied before she could speak. Not that she planned to deny it, as she had no other explanation.

Another siren sounded in the distance, drawing closer.

"That'll be Dad." Tessa turned to watch for his arrival.

He exited his SUV and joined them. He didn't speak but ran his concerned gaze over her. The first words out of his mouth would likely include calling her Peanut. She couldn't let that happen with Seth around. He'd smirk, and Braden would likely join him.

She preempted it by giving her dad a hug. "Before you ask, I really am fine."

He enveloped her in a bear hug, and when he released her, he shoved out a hand for Braden. "Looks like I'm beholden to you again."

"Glad to help."

He turned to Seth. "So where do we stand?"

Seth gave a concise update, and Tessa was impressed with the way he handled himself under her father's intense scrutiny.

"As soon as we get the issue of Tessa's safety resolved," Seth continued, "I'll canvass neighbors to see if they saw anything."

Her father planted his hands on his waist. "Consider the issue settled. I'll be escorting Tessa home."

"No. Wait," Tessa protested. "I should collect the firecracker residue."

"I'll get Natalie to do it."

"But I'm—"

"The best," he finished for her. "I know, but Natalie can get the job done. With firecrackers being illegal in the county, we're not likely to trace them back to the source, anyway."

She frowned at him. Not only because at her age she didn't want him to still have so much control in her life, but also because he was right.

Harley stepped around the corner and joined them. "This is an awful end to the day."

"Agreed," Braden said. "And it's not over. Whoever tossed those firecrackers had to know Tessa would be heading out to the pens. Which meant he was in the arena when we talked."

"He didn't sign in, I can tell you that," Tessa said. "Nana takes her role as gatekeeper seriously, and she would have followed up with anyone who snuck out a side gate and didn't sign out."

"Still, I'll want Matt to have a copy of that log to review," Walt said to Harley.

Harley nodded. "I'll get it to him the minute we finish rounding up the horses."

"I don't think we need to look beyond the side gate that was left open." Braden explained the gate issue to the others. "Since Douglas Peters was responsible for locking up, we need to talk to him first."

"Matt can follow up with him," Walt said.

Tessa frowned. "I may be the forensic person here, but I want to look Douglas in the eyes and question him."

"Now, Tessa," her dad said.

"I have to do this, Dad. You understand that, right? I mean, if someone was gunning for you, you wouldn't sit back and watch. You'd want to show them that they couldn't make you back down."

He eyed her for what seemed an eternity before he cleared his throat. "Run everything past Matt, and if he's okay with it, I'm good with you being involved. Though I'm sure he'll want you to wait until he gets this scene processed to talk to the guy, so it won't likely happen until tomorrow."

She nodded but was honestly surprised her father had acquiesced so quickly.

"I need to go help with the horses." Harley started to walk away, then turned back. "Almost forgot. Braden, there's a transport truck out front for you."

"Oh, man." Braden clamped a hand on the back of his neck. "With all the excitement, I totally forgot my horse is being delivered tonight. As part of my PR gig, I'll be riding him in the parade on Sunday."

Her father faced Braden. "Why don't you bring the horse out to our ranch? I'm not bad-mouthing the boarding here at all, but our ranch has superior facilities and your horse will have more room to roam."

"I don't want to impose," Braden said, but Tessa could tell he was considering it.

"The least I can do to repay you for saving Tessa—twice now—is to board your horse at Trails End while you're in town," her father said. "Besides, my dad will be happy to have another horse to help with. He likes keeping busy."

Tessa didn't want another connection to Braden and thought to argue, but her father was right. The horse would be better off at the ranch and doing the right thing for horses was a priority to her. And she owed Braden so much that she wanted him to feel good about where he stabled his horse, too.

"Then I accept," Braden said.

"Good. It's all settled." Her father clapped his hands. "Tessa, give your keys to Braden. He can follow us home, and the carrier can bring up the rear. We can delve into this incident over dessert and see if we can get a jump on things before another attempt is made on your life."

Braden followed the sheriff under a wide sign that read *Trails End* and started down the ranch's driveway. At the end of the long drive, he spotted a large corral abutting a big barn and stable to his right, all lit with large outside lights. Farther up the hill sat an impressive house with a welcoming glow illuminating the windows. Just the kind of place where he would have expected the McKades to live. Was he putting this fine family on a pedestal? They had to have their differences and challenges, too.

Walt parked near the house, and Tessa hopped down from the SUV. She waved Braden down a cutoff leading toward the corral. The carrier followed. She jogged along the drive, and by the time he exited her truck, she'd straddled the fence, looking so at home and at peace there that he envied her sense of homecoming. He'd never known what homecoming felt like. He'd lived in so many different apartments growing up that he never really had anything permanent enough to call home. At least not a storybook place like this. As a kid he'd always wanted to live in a house instead of ratty apartments, but it didn't take long for him to realize it was a fairy-tale dream, and the chances of finding it was so minuscule that he'd let it go.

The carrier driver gave Braden a rundown on how the trip had gone before opening the trailer door so Braden could step in with Shadow.

"Hey there, Shadow." Braden moved to the

front of the trailer and, with slight pressure on Shadow's chest, urged him to back out of the carrier. Shadow easily complied, and Braden had to admit the many hours he'd spent training Shadow on trailering had paid off.

Under the bright exterior lights, he checked Shadow for injuries, and finding none, he signed the paperwork and led Shadow to Tessa, who eyed them with interest. Behind her, a sorrel horse strolled toward the fence. Copper, Braden knew, as he remembered the distinct marking on the horse's face.

"Well, hello, handsome fella," Tessa said to Shadow as she slid down from the rail. "I assume since his ears are up and pointed forward that he's okay with being touched by a stranger."

Braden nodded. "Shadow hasn't met a person he doesn't like."

She put out her hand, and Shadow sniffed, then nudged her with his nose. "You *are* a big softy, aren't you?"

She rubbed his neck for a moment before looking up at Braden. But Shadow refused to let her ignore him and shoved his head back under her hand. She laughed, a delightful sound that warmed Braden's heart, and he smiled along with her. The horse behind her bumped his head into her back, shoving her forward. She turned to look at him.

"Not cool, Copper," she scolded. "I know you're jealous, but that doesn't mean you can have bad manners."

Copper whinnied, and she stepped away. Some people might think she was being cruel to Copper, but she was showing him that she was the boss and an aggressive move like head butting wasn't acceptable.

"Why don't we show Shadow where the water is, and we can turn him out in the empty corral." She didn't wait for Braden's agreement but headed through the stable to a water trough on the far side of the building. He let Shadow drink his fill of water, then bent to remove the travel boots that kept the horse's legs safe while in the carrier. He removed the halter and released Shadow to explore his new home.

Tessa closed the gate. "Nana's expecting us, but if we have time later, maybe we can introduce him to Copper to see how they get along."

He heard the doubt in her tone, and as he followed her up to the house, he had to wonder why. With all the traveling and rodeos, Copper must get on well with other horses. She didn't know Shadow, so maybe she was thinking of his temperament. Or maybe she believed the horses would pick up on the tension between them and be ill at ease with each other.

On the porch, she swiped her boots over a

scraper before entering. He followed suit. A bouncing black Lab and a tall, slender woman with dishwater-blond hair falling to her shoulders greeted them in the foyer. Though Tessa didn't share this woman's features, Tessa had the same strong stance, and so he had to assume this was her mother.

"Mom, this is Braden Hayes," Tessa said, confirming his suspicions, as she dropped down to the floor and hugged the shiny-coated Lab. "Braden. My mother, Winnie."

She crossed over to him. "If you're adverse to hugging, let me know now, as I plan to give you one for rescuing my baby not only once but two times now."

Braden had never been much of a hugger, but there was something compelling about these McKade women that made him want to let them hug him. He smiled. "Bring it on."

She wrapped her long arms around his neck and held him tightly like a mother bear welcoming her little cub home. If he didn't know better, he'd think she realized he'd missed out on such affection growing up, but that was impossible, right?

She pushed back and glanced at the doorway. "I don't see your suitcase." She spun to look at her husband, who was entering the foyer. "Tell me you remembered to invite Braden to stay with us while he's in town."

"I…well… I remembered to invite his horse."

Winnie's hands went to her hips. "Walt McKade. I don't know what to do with you sometimes."

His face colored, and Braden liked seeing that the strong lawman had multiple sides to his personality.

She spun to face Braden. "We would be most honored if you would stay here on the ranch. If you don't want a room in the house with the wild McKade clan, you're welcome to one of the cabins we use for the dude ranch."

"I…" he said. He automatically began to turn her down, thinking it would be too much of an imposition. But then he really thought about the offer. He was surprised to find that he wanted to stay with them. Especially to be near Tessa, but the McKade family dynamics so fascinated him, he wanted more of that, too.

"It's okay," Tessa said from her position on the floor with the dog. "You won't be hurting our feelings if you want to go back to your motel."

She sounded most eager for him to refuse, and that made him want to accept even more.

Her father eyed her. "I may have failed to offer the invitation, but now that it's out there, he's staying here."

"But, Dad," Tessa said, coming to her feet. The dog shot up with her, its head tilted and alert.

Walt held up a hand. "No buts, Peanut. This man has come to your rescue twice, and we are beholden to him. Besides, the latest incident reinforces our need of an extra set of eyes on you at all times."

"I'd be glad to accept your hospitality, Sheriff," Braden said before Tessa argued again.

With a swift nod by her father, the subject was closed, and Tessa's frown declared how much she hated the decision.

EIGHT

Ten place settings sat around the long oak dining table. The sheer size of the table made Braden's steps falter. Was he really ready to face so much of the McKade clan all at one time? He had no experience with families like this one. Butterflies he hadn't felt since the first time he climbed on a bull tumbled through his stomach.

"Don't look so worried." Winnie bumped through the adjoining kitchen door carrying a tray of glasses and a pitcher of ice water. "You've faced some mighty fierce bulls. You can handle a few McKades."

Could he?

"Let me put these out for you." He took the tray from her and set it on the table.

Tessa stepped into the room, the black Lab trailing her.

Her mother faced Tessa. "He's strong. Courageous. *And* he has manners. You might want to take note of that."

Tessa groaned, and Winnie departed with a wide smile on her face. The dog padded over to Braden, and he knelt down to scratch her shiny black head. He'd always wanted a pet, but his parents hadn't been able to afford one, nor would they have taken care of one. And now, he worked such long hours, it wouldn't be fair to an animal.

Tessa dropped onto a chair. "Do you get the same thing from your family, too?"

"You mean the not-so-subtle matchmaking?"

She nodded.

"No."

"Oh, wait… I didn't think… You must have a girlfriend already." Her face turned the color of her hair.

"No," he said again and was about to explain when the front door burst open and chattering people entered the house. He expected the dog to start barking, but she simply tilted her head again as if taking things in.

"Your dog is well behaved," he said.

"You are, aren't you, Echo?" Tessa smiled lovingly at the dog. "She was training to be a helper dog for the hearing impaired, but her temperament was too feisty. She washed out of the program, and I adopted her a few months ago. I've continued her obedience training, and she's a real joy."

Braden tried to focus on Echo as her tongue

came out to lick his face, but the group in the foyer took his attention. He recognized Matt, Kendall and Gavin, who had his arm around a woman wearing worn red boots with her jeans. Tessa went out to greet them. Braden didn't want to intrude, but he listened to the conversation, mostly revolving around concern for Tessa's well-being.

He grew more unsettled and couldn't sit. He patted Echo's head, then stood to fill the glasses with water.

Matt broke off from the group and came into the room. "You two have become friends awful fast."

"Tessa?" Braden shot her a look as if he could see on her face what she'd said to her brother to make him think such a thing.

"Echo," Matt said. "I meant Echo."

"Oh, the dog."

"She's a friendly little thing but rarely gives anyone else attention when Tessa's around." Matt arched a brow as if waiting for Braden to comment, but he didn't have a clue what to say.

"So we're indebted to you yet one more time," Matt said. "I hope it doesn't become a habit. Not the having you around part, but the rescuing Tessa because she's still in danger part."

Braden gave a firm nod of understanding and

filled a glass with water as the family descended on the room.

"You told me he was good-looking, Kendall, but he does chores, too?" The other woman tossed her blond hair over her shoulder and looked up at Gavin with an impish grin. "Is it too late for an annulment?"

Gavin growled and pulled her to his side. "Braden, this is my wife, Lexie. At least until after dessert." He chuckled and kissed the top of her head.

She turned her attention to Braden. "You should definitely sit by me, since we're the only non-McKades in the group."

"Um, honey," Gavin said, "you're a McKade now, too."

"I meant we're the only ones not born into this crazy family." She chuckled.

The kitchen door swung open, and Winnie entered holding a golden-brown blueberry pie.

"Sit," she commanded.

Walt and Jed joined them and settled at the ends of the table, a nearby seat left open for their wives.

"Can I help with anything?" Braden asked Winnie, as he was starting to feel uncomfortable about everyone seeming to know where to sit, while he had no clue what to do.

"Thank you, but Betty and I do this all the time, and we have things under control."

"The kitchen is their domain," Tessa said. "They always turn down offers of help, so we've stopped asking. Now, doing dishes is another story."

Braden made note of that and waited for everyone to sit before taking the chair between Tessa and Lexie. Winnie returned with another pie followed by Betty with a pot of coffee and mugs. When the women had taken a seat and Walt had said grace, Betty began cutting the pie and Winnie poured the coffee for those who requested it.

Tessa took a bite of her pie, the berries oozing out, and she groaned. "No one makes pie like you, Nana."

She waved away the comment. "I'm sure Braden had his share of good home cooking growing up."

"Nothing this good," he said and left it at that. He wasn't going to drag down the mood of the group with talk about his upbringing that involved zero home-baked goods.

Matt dropped a fork to his plate. "I need to get back to the arena to check in with Natalie, but I'd like to run down the leads in the investigation before I go."

Normally, Braden would have appreciated Matt's single-minded focus, but he was enjoying the family atmosphere and hated to have it ruined by the reminder of the reason he was there.

"I wish for once we could enjoy a nice dessert without all the law enforcement talk," Betty grumbled.

Jed looked at his wife for a long moment. "That's not like you, sweetheart. Something wrong?"

She sighed. "No…it's just…there *is* life outside of law enforcement, but you'd never know it by our family meals. I know finding this suspect is top priority. No one wants to make sure our Tessa is safe more than me, but can we wait until after dessert to talk about it?"

Kendall gasped, but when Braden looked at her, he saw she was joking. "What do you want to talk about, Nana?"

"The dude ranch is a safe topic," she suggested.

Braden latched on to that comment, as he was eager to know more about the family business. "I saw the sign when I drove up. Who's in charge of it?"

Tessa set down her fork. "We all pitch in. Granddad and Nana do most of the physical work. Kendall manages the reservations and the website. Mom and Dad handle the finances, and I take care of the horse activities with the guests. Matt's in charge of special events."

"Lexie and I have just gotten involved, pitching in wherever needed," Gavin added.

"And we're glad to have you." Betty smiled at the couple, then turned her gaze on Matt before moving on to Kendall and settling on Tessa. "We can always use help, so I'd like to think if the rest of my grandchildren sitting at this table decide to get married, that their spouses will be like Lexie and embrace the ranch."

A knowing look passed between Tessa and her siblings. It wasn't hard to see they wished Betty wouldn't hint at marriage so often. But honestly, Braden liked that someone even cared enough to think about their future. Except for the money they wanted to borrow from him, his parents didn't care one lick about what happened to him, much less if he got married. In fact, if they would ever talk about it, he was sure after their miserable failures, they'd discourage him from even considering marriage.

"So, back to the investigation." Matt wiped his fingers on a gingham-checked napkin. "We know we're looking for a male with shoes about a size ten, maybe a bull rider who wears a pink vest. Harley said Falby's the only guy in the area with a pink vest, but I'll review the files I pulled on Tessa's prior arrests to see if we have a bull rider in the group. And I'm going to have a talk with each of these guys tomorrow."

"Did you have a chance to talk to Ernie Winston to see if the pink leather is from one of his employees?" Braden asked.

"We've been playing phone tag," Matt replied. "I did question Vic, though, about who hit him. The guy came up from behind while he was securing the gate for the night, and he didn't get a look at him."

"Anything else we know?" Gavin asked.

Matt nodded. "Harley sent Yancy Tate in for elimination fingerprints, and Natalie got his card to the print examiner."

"Did Perry Richter show up?" Tessa asked.

"No."

"Then we'll have to follow up with him."

Braden was glad that at least Tate had come in. Maybe with his prints and Harley's, they'd be able to narrow things down to a viable suspect. "Has anyone contacted Jason to see if he's in town?"

"Jason?" Winnie sat forward. "You can't possibly think he would be behind this."

"We have to check out every possibility, Mom," Matt said.

"I've been trying to get ahold of him, but he's not returning my calls." Kendall set down her water glass. "Not surprising with how he and Tessa left things."

Braden glanced at Tessa, who clenched her jaw.

Matt swallowed his bite. "I got the arena sign-in sheet from Harley and reviewed it. Everyone signed out, which is no surprise, since Nana was in charge."

A murmur of agreement traveled around the table, and Betty smiled at her family, her eyes aglow with love for them. To Braden, she seemed like the perfect grandmother, but he wouldn't let that distract him right now.

"Our suspect doesn't need to have signed in," he said, and all family members swung their gazes to stare at him. He felt the force of the family's strength focused on him but didn't let it rattle him. "I'm not trying to criticize rodeo security, but there was a side gate left open. Anyone could've slipped through it. I mentioned it to Harley, and he's assured me that he'll take care of it going forward, but that doesn't help us figure out who might have used it already."

Walt looked over his coffee mug. "If Harley says he'll take care of something, he will. That gate won't be a problem anymore."

Braden nodded. "But I know you won't take offense if I ask you to have your deputies check all the gates on routine patrols. And of course, I'll check them out whenever I'm at the arena."

"I'd expect nothing less." Walt smiled. "You're sure living up to your lieutenant's assessment. If you ever find yourself moving to our county, I'd be honored to have a man like you on my team."

A job offer. Most unexpected. Braden quickly glanced at Tessa to see her reaction.

She was spinning her water glass between her fingers, staring at the rings she'd left in the condensation. "I'll head to the lab in the morning to review any evidence Natalie collects tonight and see if I can find a good lead."

Braden shouldn't have read anything into her avoidance of responding to her father's job offer, but how could he not? She still wanted nothing to do with him and here he was enjoying her family and coming to like her more than he should.

"Are you free to accompany Tessa to the lab?" Walt asked.

Braden didn't even have to think about his answer and nodded.

She may not like the thought of having him in her life, but he couldn't let that bother him. Not when he couldn't stomach the thought of anything bad happening to her. Several publicity events were on his schedule tomorrow, but he'd reschedule them. There was no way he'd let her leave the ranch without him by her side.

With dessert winding down, Tessa felt antsy. The family often came together for dinner or dessert at the end of a busy day. Normally, they adjourned to the family room afterward. With Braden here, she wondered if that would happen.

She had to admit she enjoyed watching him interact with her family. Until her dad's bombshell about a job. What was he thinking? He barely even knew Braden. But her dad was a good judge of character, and he seemed to like Braden. Not like the few guys she'd dated in the past, though he'd never let on that he'd distrusted Jason.

She'd rarely invited a guy to meet the family—and Braden wasn't a guy in that sense—and of the few men she had brought home, most succumbed to her father's careful watch and clammed up. Jason hadn't and now Braden didn't seem a bit fazed by her dad, either. In hindsight, she could see Jason's refusal to be rattled came from thinking he was superior to most men, but Braden's came from a quiet sense of confidence, and he fit right in. He was relaxed and joined in their jokes but had a serious side that said he was keeping watch over her.

He pushed his blueberry-stained plate away. "It's a good thing I don't live here or I'd have a serious weight issue."

Tessa couldn't imagine that he'd let himself gain weight. He must work out. Not that she was checking him out or anything.

"I'd be glad to help with the dishes," he offered.

Nana didn't say a word but fired a pointed look at Tessa.

Tessa couldn't decide if her grandmother was

noting that he was a good guy or asking Tessa to save him from washing dishes. She chose to believe the second one. "I think we should check on Shadow."

"And you need to get your things from the motel," her mother added to Braden.

"Go check on Shadow." Nana made a shooing motion with her hands. "It's a beautiful night. The stars are out in full force. Take your time. Enjoy them."

Tessa got up before Nana had her and Braden walking down the aisle. Since Gavin had married such a wonderful woman, her grandmother had become obsessed with matchmaking her remaining grandchildren.

Echo met Tessa in the foyer, and when Braden joined them, they all stepped outside.

"Betty was right." He planted his feet and stared up at the sky, seeming content for the first time since Tessa had run into him again.

Moonlight danced across his face, highlighting his angular jaw, and Tessa couldn't look away from his handsome silhouette. She admired his rugged masculinity, her heart starting to thump faster.

He lowered his head. Caught her gaze and smiled. She snapped her gaze to the sky, heat flushing up her neck at being caught gawking. She held her breath as she waited for him to comment.

"I always forget how clear it is out in the country and how many stars God put in the sky," he said, and she let out her breath. "I've been thinking. I told you how I got into bull riding, but you never mentioned how you started barrel racing."

"How does anyone get started in such a thing?" she said to avoid a personal conversation when her heart was so vulnerable to him.

"Most of the time rodeoing runs in the family," he pressed. "The parents are hooked, and then the kids get hooked. 'Course, that didn't happen to me, and that's not the way it is in your case, right? At least, I don't remember hearing about another McKade involved in the rodeo."

"I'm the only one." She started toward the corral and hoped he wouldn't keep probing.

Copper waited at the fence, so she stopped to rub his neck. Braden sidled up next to her. His shoulder bumped hers, firing off her nerve endings. She started to move away, but she wasn't about to let him know how his closeness impacted her, so she remained riveted in place.

"So what drew you to barrel racing?" he asked.

She didn't want to share, but as he'd said, he'd told her about his bull riding. It was only fair for her to reciprocate. "I liked spending time with Copper. I figured barrel racing would give me a chance to do more of that."

"But couldn't you simply spend time with him here on the ranch?"

She shook her head. "Mom and Dad would've told me I was wasting time and put me to work. When I was away at competitions, they thought I was socializing and so it was okay."

"Socializing? You lost me." His questioning gaze burned into her.

She found herself wanting to answer but couldn't keep looking at him. She turned back to Copper. "I was so shy—nothing like my siblings. They were all outgoing. Still are. I found socializing awkward and scary. So I kept to myself. Spent time with Copper or went running. Mom and Dad tried to get me involved elsewhere, but it didn't feel right. Hanging with Copper did. Even competing with him. We got attention in the arena, but I could handle it by focusing on the riding."

"So that's why you didn't join in with the rest of us back then."

She spun to look at him. "I don't get why you even noticed me. I sure wasn't like the rodeo princesses that you usually were seen spending time with."

He met her gaze and held it, and she felt the full force of his interest in her. The night was silent, and she could only hear her heart beating.

It was just the two of them and the temptation to run her finger along that scar came rushing back.

"There was something in your eyes," he said softly, his gaze never wavering. "The way you watched everyone around you. Not like you wanted to be part of the group and felt left out. More like you were trying to figure out what made us tick."

She had to look away from him or she'd cave in to the urge to touch him. "My mom always thought I had to be lonely, but I wasn't. Not really. I had Copper and my family. And as you just saw, they can be overwhelming. That was enough for me. I'm still an introvert. Unless you want to talk about forensics. Then I'm glad to blab on and on."

"And are you lonely now?"

If he meant right this minute, not at all. But otherwise, was she?

"I don't know," she whispered.

"I hope not," he said. "I'd like to think you're happy and have everything you want in life." He turned a heart-stopping smile on her that said he totally got her.

Never had a guy looked at her like this before. Not even Jason. *Remember Jason*, she told herself.

She turned away and headed to Shadow's corral, her heart now heavy from the realization that this man who was off-limits was also a guy who stirred her emotions, and she found him very compelling.

She let out a shuddering breath and searched for Shadow. He stood on the far side of the corral, lifted his head to look at her. If it had been Copper, he would have come running, but Shadow didn't move. Not even when Braden stepped up beside her.

"So how long have you owned Shadow?" she asked, hoping to keep things on the safe subject of horses.

"I bought him after I retired from bull riding." His tone was wistful.

Echo trotted over to him, and he sank down on a straw bale to ruffle her ears, the same look of longing Tessa had seen at the arena darkening his gaze. "I missed the whole rodeo scene. Thought maybe owning a horse would help make up for it."

"And did it?"

"Yeah… I mean, some." He rested his corded forearms on his knees and let Echo lick the side of his face.

She couldn't believe Echo was warming up to him so quickly. Obviously, he attracted females of all kinds.

"The adrenaline rush isn't there when riding

Shadow," he continued. "But doing these special appearances helps me relive the glory days."

"Why quit at the peak of your game?"

He didn't answer for the longest time but finally shook his head. "Family complications."

His tone had changed. He'd closed down and wasn't going to elaborate.

She should respect his boundaries, but he'd just probed into her past and turnabout was fair play. "What kind of issues?"

"Finances." His tone warned her not to keep questioning.

She ignored it. "I saw your winnings. So it couldn't have been lack of money, right?"

"It's not something I'm comfortable talking about." He raised his head. The warmth was gone from his expression and it was now closed and dark.

She wanted nothing more than to know what he was hiding, but she could sense she'd pushed him too far. She'd lay off for now. If they spent much more time together, she'd get to the bottom of it eventually. Of that, he could be sure.

NINE

Tessa didn't know what she expected from Douglas the next morning when she knocked on his front door. She desperately wanted him to be guilty, so she hoped she could be objective, as she'd promised Matt she would be.

Douglas answered the door. He was wearing jeans, an ironed T-shirt that strained at his biceps and a deep frown. "Well, if it isn't the famous Braden Hayes and Tessa McKade."

Tessa was already tired of the guy's attitude, so she decided not to ease into the questions. "Why did you leave the gate open last night?"

"Gate?" Douglas asked. "What gate?"

"The side one at the arena. Harley said it was your responsibility to secure all of the gates last night."

He stared at Tessa, his gaze shifty at best. "Guess I missed one. No biggie. Nothing to steal in that place, anyway."

Tessa crossed her arms. "Give this innocent act a rest already."

"I'm not—"

"I was almost trampled by broncs at the arena last night," she interrupted and gave him details to watch his reaction.

He simply looked at her. "So that's why Matt came by to search my truck last night."

Braden's eyebrows rose. "Matt didn't give you a reason and you let him search anyway?"

"I pestered him, sure, but when he wouldn't talk about it, I gave in. After all, I have nothing to hide."

Tessa doubted that.

"We're making progress in investigating the bull theft, and we know you're involved," Braden stated.

Tessa glanced at him in surprise, as they knew no such thing, but he was likely hoping it would get Douglas to tell them the truth.

Douglas's face paled, and he took a step back. His face had guilt written all over it. Just a little more pressure and he might confess.

"Come clean on your part in the theft, and we'll ask the DA to go easy on you," Tessa added.

His mouth dropped open. Panic flared in his eyes. He darted his gaze around, looking for an escape route. He suddenly shot forward, pushing between them. He charged down the steps and bolted away.

Tessa took off in pursuit. Douglas might have longer legs, but he was all muscle-bound and not a runner like her. She'd reacted faster than Braden had and beat him off the stoop. He was just now catching up, but Douglas was nearly to his truck, and she wouldn't let him get away.

She flew through the air, grabbed Douglas's shoulders and took him down. They hit the ground with a bone-jarring thud. She landed on top of him, and he tried to buck her off. No way she'd let that happen. In a flash, she had her knee in his back, wrenching his arms around to subdue him.

She heard Braden arrive, but she didn't need his help to handle Douglas. She tightened her hold on his wrists. "Knock it off, Douglas, or I'll charge you with resisting arrest."

He stopped struggling. "You never said you were arresting me."

"Never said I wasn't," she fired back at him. "Can you sit up and have a civilized conversation, or do I need to get my cuffs from the truck and haul you in?"

"I'll talk," he mumbled under his breath.

"You so much as hint at standing, and I'll cuff you." She let him go and came to her feet to tower over him as he scooted back to rest against a tire. "Let's start with you telling us why you ran."

"I panicked."

"Yeah, I got that. But why?"

"The bull." He paused to gnaw on his lower lip. "I might… Maybe something I said made it happen."

Did he just confess to his involvement? Tessa could hardly believe it. She'd highly suspected him, even wanted him to be guilty, but now that he was admitting it, she was shocked and could only gape at him.

"Explain," Braden demanded.

"A while back, I was at Duke's bar."

"Country Western bar in town," Tessa told Braden. "Has a bad reputation for brawls."

"So what happened at Duke's?" Braden asked.

"Had a drink or two." Douglas eyed her. "Someone mentioned the rodeo and kept going on and on about how this would be your tenth year winning. I told him Felicia was a better racer and deserved to be recognized. He just laughed and walked away. I got mad. She's my sister, and I'm tired of everything always coming easy to the McKades when the rest of us have to work hard to succeed."

Tessa scoffed. Nothing but spite and jealousy could make anyone believe the McKades didn't work hard.

"So you were mad," Braden said to Douglas, keeping them on track.

"Yeah, and I didn't let it go. You know...kept bending the bartender's ear. After a while, this guy at the bar slides down next to me and says he can help me out. He just needed a little information, and he could make my wishes for Felicia come true. He knew I was in charge of the bull schedule, and if I could give him the name of the earliest bull to check in, he'd do the rest."

"So you told him about King Slammer at nine?" Braden asked.

"Sort of." Douglas got a sick look on his face. "He was originally on the schedule for nine, but this guy asked me if I could get King Slammer dropped off earlier. So I agreed to ask the owner to have the bull at the arena by seven. I didn't change the official schedule, though. If I did, Harley would've started asking questions. I just planned to tell him they got confused about the time."

"Official schedule or not, this guy knew exactly when King Slammer would be on the road so he could steal the bull," Tessa said and couldn't keep the disgust from her tone.

Douglas held up his hands like he was afraid she would slap on those cuffs. "Yeah, but I didn't know that at the time. And I sure didn't have any idea what he planned to do with the information."

He swung his head in a sorrowful arc. "You gotta believe me. I didn't know he'd try to kill anyone."

"But you didn't ask what he planned to do, did you?" Braden asked, his fingers curling into fists.

Douglas cringed. "Hey, man. I was drunk. I don't know half the things I did or didn't do that night. You know what it's like to be drunk."

"Unfortunately, I do, from the other side," Braden replied. "From arresting men like you who drink too much and commit crimes."

Douglas looked annoyed, and his chin came up as if he planned to argue.

Tessa wouldn't give him the chance. "Who was this man?"

"I don't know. He didn't give his name."

"Describe him, then."

"I was too drunk. I don't remember."

Braden stepped closer. "You telling the truth about that, or do we have to haul you in for further questioning?"

Douglas held up his hands. "Hey, man. It's the truth. I swear."

The enormity of what he'd done all because he wanted his sister to win finally hit Tessa. "I can't believe you'd do this."

"Like I said, I didn't know what the guy was going to do with King Slammer."

If Tessa had publicly announced her retirement, maybe none of this would have happened as any competitor who wanted her gone might have accepted that this was the last year she could win and the next year the spot could be theirs. Or would it have? Their suspect had proved his tenacity. Even if he didn't have Douglas's help, and with him likely having his own reasons for targeting her, he would have figured out a way to steal the bull or another way to try to kill her.

Braden pushed back his chair at the McKade's outdoor dining table. He'd brought Tessa home for a dinner of salad, baked potatoes and thick steaks grilled to perfection by Walt. Winnie had scheduled an early dinner so Tessa could digest her food long before the competition.

Braden wished they were closer to finding the suspect, but after spending the rest of the day at the lab and stopping to interview the bartender at Duke's, they'd learned nothing new. Sure, the bartender confirmed that Douglas had indeed bad-mouthed Tessa and a guy had chatted with him for a long time about the bull, but unfortunately the bartender didn't know the man and didn't remember what he looked like.

So another dead end. Not unusual in an investigation, but still frustrating.

A strong breeze played over the shaded area, making the stifling heat almost bearable. If danger to Tessa wasn't still foremost in Braden's mind, he could honestly say he'd feel at peace here. Having grown up in the city where he didn't know his neighbors, he'd never experienced the wonderful sense of community that he'd found with the McKades, and that he could easily imagine existed in Lost Creek. He had to admit he liked it and could get used to living in a place where others looked out for one another. Get used to family like this by his side.

Maybe he should consider Walt's job offer. But why? He loved his detective job in Austin. He had no desire to leave it.

Echo trotted over and looked up at him with big puppy eyes. He scratched her head, and she placed it on his knee.

"She likes you," Betty said as she passed by with a platter of empty watermelon rinds. "And she's not the only one. You fit in nicely with all of us."

Did he? He took a good look at the family seated in various lawn chairs, relaxed and chatting. Winnie had taken him aside before dinner and said that with Tessa's upcoming competition, the family wanted her to relax, and they'd all agreed to avoid discussing the attempts on her life.

He'd experienced their intensity before now—their drive and desire to protect the town and find the man who wanted to hurt one of their own—

but this family, the people in front of him tonight who were joking and just enjoying each other, was a sight to behold.

What would life have been like growing up under the strong wings of Walt and Winnie, and Betty and Jed? Braden's take on marriage would surely be different. Still, he was smart enough to know that most families weren't like the McKades and marriage was still a great risk. If it wasn't, the divorce rate wouldn't be so high.

Would it be a risk with Tessa?

He watched her as she laughed with her siblings. He probably looked like a lovesick teenager, because he was feeling like one. After seeing his parents' failed relationship, he'd never wanted a serious relationship, so he hadn't let himself fall for a woman. But here he was quickly tumbling head over heels for this one particular woman, who often looked at him like she'd choose a passel of rattlesnakes over him.

Seriously. Stop it.

He had to get away for a few minutes before he came to believe a life like this was actually possible for a guy like him, who didn't really even know what love was.

He eased Echo's head off his leg. "Sorry to eat and run, but I want to spend a few minutes with Shadow before we go."

He nearly bolted from his chair, and he'd never

run from anything in his life. Even the scary nights as a kid panhandling on a corner. Deep down, despite his protests, he wanted a family like the McKades. Had always wanted that. Imagined it as a boy. That someone would swoop in and take him away. Be there for him and love him the way other kids in his classes were loved. He couldn't pinpoint when he'd let that dream go. Maybe when he was old enough to start dating. Old enough to realize how forming a relationship when he wasn't any good at it would ensure he'd end up like his parents. He'd rather be alone than have that.

Is that what God wants for you?

Wait, where did that come from? He'd never consulted God about relationships. No point, or so he'd thought. Had he left God out because he was afraid of what He might tell him?

Braden approached Shadow and patted his neck. Lingered for a long time and felt like giving him a hug. How absurd. He'd never hugged his horse. He was losing it.

"You took off mighty fast," Tessa said from behind him, her voice a balm for his aching heart.

"We've been so busy that I've neglected Shadow." He spoke the truth, but still, it felt like a lie as he turned. She'd changed into a purple plaid shirt and clean jeans, her belt holding a championship buckle. She'd settled her white hat on her head, hiding her amazing red hair.

"Seemed like more than that to me." She met his gaze and held it.

If he kept looking at her, he might blurt out his feelings and where would that get him? Nowhere. Better to keep them at bay. He grabbed a brush to groom Shadow.

"I hope it's not my family who put you off," she said.

"I like your family and have come to see how amazing they are."

She arched a brow. "We're just a regular old family. Nothing special."

"You say that because you didn't grow up in a dysfunctional family like I did." Shocked that he'd voluntarily brought up his past, he turned his attention back to Shadow.

"Tell me about them." Her tone was soft and encouraging.

His first thought was to blow off her request, but she'd been open and honest with him about her childhood with Copper, and he'd already left her hanging over questions about his life once before. He wanted to reciprocate now, but he couldn't get a word out.

"Braden?" she prompted.

"Nothing much to tell," he said, stating the only thing he felt comfortable saying.

"What do they do for a living?"

Yeah, what do they do?

She laid a hand on his shoulder and urged him to look at her. When he did, the tenderness in her eyes broke him. He couldn't remember anyone ever looking at him like that. How could he refuse to share when he wanted more of that look?

"They didn't much like working and usually found a way to live off the welfare system," he said matter-of-factly, but his gut was churning. "Honestly, they didn't much like doing anything—including being parents. But I got more of their attention once I was old enough to do things for them."

"Do things? Like what?"

Memories came flying back like a bad dream. He swallowed hard. "I fetched whatever they wanted whenever they wanted it. A cigarette. A cocktail they taught me to mix. Groceries from the store. Money for the rent."

She gaped at him. "Rent? But you were a kid. How'd you do that?"

She wasn't holding him there. He could walk away and end this conversation. But he remembered her compassion and stayed rooted in place. "I stood on a street corner with a sign. Was told not to come home until bedtime and not to come home at all if I hadn't gotten enough cash." He shuddered at the memory and couldn't believe he'd told her.

Her shocked expression was the reason he hadn't wanted to share in the first place. "That's horrible. You were just a kid. How did you get through it?"

"Honestly, it wasn't bad when I was little. Sure, when it got dark, I was afraid. But it was worse when I got into middle school. I didn't care when I was little when other kids saw me, but as a teen. Man, I've never been so humiliated."

He saw her hand curl into a fist. "Why didn't you report your parents?"

He shrugged. "It was just my way of life back then. I didn't know anything else."

"And no one thought to report a little kid pan-handling on his own?"

"That was a long time ago. Things were different. Maybe people reported us, but my parents never told me if they did. Besides, if they had, we weren't easy to track down. We were evicted all the time, and we moved from one low-rent dump to the next."

Fire burned in her eyes, and she shook her head sorrowfully. "I still don't know if my family is all that unique, but I do know your parents were guilty of child abuse. I'd like to arrest them and throw away the key."

He'd never had anyone come to his defense so

fiercely, and warmth spread through his heart. It was probably nothing special to her, and he shouldn't put much stock in it. He was sure most people would react in a similar way if he ever shared his story, but part of him wanted to think her defense was more personal—that she was concerned about *him* and not just the hardships he'd faced.

He smiled. "Thanks for caring so much."

"I support the people I care about."

His turn to gape at her. "You care about me?"

"Well…yeah… I mean, you saved my life. How could I not?" Her face colored as he was coming to know it often did.

Her reaction sure seemed like it was more than just gratitude, but again, he shouldn't be reading too much into her response and needed to end this conversation.

"What time do you need to be at the arena?" he asked.

She glanced at her watch. "I need to get Copper loaded up now."

"Can I help?"

"I've got it," she said. "And you wanted to spend time with Shadow."

She started to walk away when her phone rang. She glanced at the screen, and her face lit up. "Our fingerprint analyst. Maybe Falby's prints matched the ones on the lock.

"Randy," she answered. "Please tell me you have something for me."

She listened carefully, her mouth soon turning down. Braden's protective instincts had him dropping the brush on the shelf and stepping over to her.

"You're sure?" She bit her lower lip, then released it in a long sigh. "Okay, thanks, Randy."

Braden didn't wait for her to share the conversation. "Bad news I take it."

"Randy ran the prints from the lock. One of them matched Harley, one had no match, but the third came back for Millard Ingram, Jr."

"Do you know this Ingram guy?"

She nodded. "He's a local who had only a sheet full of misdemeanors until I arrested him in my rookie year for felony elder abuse. He was just released this week."

"If that's the case, shouldn't he have come up on your department prison-release calendar? I'd have thought your dad would be all over him."

She nodded. "Maybe an admin made a mistake and put in the wrong date. We'll have to check with Dad."

"Tell me about Ingram."

She took a long breath. Let it out slowly. "Not much to say other than he's the lowest of the low. He abused his own grandmother. I arrested him, and he was convicted. Now he's out."

Braden didn't like hearing that this man, one who would stoop low enough to beat his grandmother, was possibly responsible for trying to hurt Tessa. He didn't like it one bit and took an instinctual step closer to her. "Would he want to come after you?"

She shrugged. "I made the arrest, but he has to know someone else would have hauled him in if I hadn't."

"Doesn't mean he doesn't want to get even."

"True, but he never threatened me."

"Is there a good explanation for why his prints are on the lock?"

"He hasn't been connected to the rodeo in years if that's what you mean, so he has no business messing with the lock, but he could still have friends in the rodeo."

"Does he have experience that would allow him to handle a bull?"

"He was raised on a cattle ranch and was a bull rider in his teens for a year or so before he started running with a rough crowd and gave it up."

Braden was starting to think this guy was a good possibility for their suspect. "Sounds like we need to talk to him. Any ideas on where to find him?"

She shook her head. "He lived with his father and grandmother on the family ranch until I arrested him."

"But he couldn't have gone back there after beating his grandmother, right?"

"Not necessarily. Even when Junior was convicted, his dad stood by him. His grandmother initially testified against Junior but then expressed remorse for turning him in and asked the prosecutor to drop the charges."

"What happened with that?"

"She'd already testified, so unless she agreed to recant her testimony and face perjury charges, the prosecutor wouldn't budge. She couldn't lie, so she let the charges stand—and the conviction that followed. But she felt responsible for him going to jail, so I could see her feeling so bad she would let him come home." Tessa glanced at her watch. "I really need to get going, but I can have Kendall check with the prison to see if he left a forwarding address."

"You load up Copper, and I'll give your family the news so they can be on the lookout for him tonight."

A pensive expression crossed her face. "Let's hold off on that until after the rodeo or they won't relax and enjoy the show."

Braden met her gaze and held it. "Let's be clear here, Tessa. I want all of them to have a good time, but not at the expense of your life."

Tessa sighed. "I know you're right. I just hate to ruin their night. Ask Kendall to send a picture of Junior to everyone's phone so we can keep an eye out for him."

He placed his hands on her shoulders and waited for her to look up at him. "Promise you won't leave without me by your side."

"I promise, but go before you make me late."

Braden took off running. He passed her truck and thought about removing her keys, but now that he'd gotten to know her, he decided to trust her promise. Felt odd, when he honestly never fully trusted anyone.

Not even God. Braden's thought from last night came rushing back. He'd come to faith when he'd started hanging out with Hal in middle school. His family was a God-fearing, Bible-toting kind of family. Their church's youth pastor had been down-to-earth and a good role model for Braden. He'd finally learned what a real father might have been like. Then he went home to his dad and saw all that was wrong with his life.

But God had gotten him out of that world with bull riding. Braden honestly believed the sport had saved his life. It took him away from his family and gave him a future. He would always be grateful for that and had put his life in God's hands. But he clearly had trust issues with God, too, and needed to be in prayer about it.

He rounded the corner of the house, and Walt shot to his feet. "What is it?"

Braden shared the latest news. "He was released a few days ago."

Walt frowned. "We've had some problems with that database since an update last week."

"I've been working on getting that sorted out," Kendall said. "But I've had other software like our fingerprint database that's more pressing."

Braden knew how that went. There was never enough of a budget to keep up with technology and fix problems. Probably even more true with a smaller county department.

Walt nodded. "Can you send Ingram's picture to our phones and put out an alert on him?"

Kendall nodded.

Braden shared his phone number with her so she could text a picture to him, as well. "I'll head back to the stable and escort Tessa into town."

"You won't be the only one on this escort," Walt said. "I'll be coming with you."

"Seth and I are on duty tonight at the arena," Matt said. "So we'll be right there with you, too."

Gavin came to his feet, his stance and expression an exact match to his father's. "I'll be there, too, and forget the rules about carrying inside the arena. I'll be strapped and watching for anyone who even looks sideways."

"Count me in on that," Jed said, reminding Braden that he was the retired sheriff.

"Can I make one observation?" Braden asked.

"Out with it," Walt snapped.

"Tessa hates the idea that this will ruin your fun night at the rodeo. So can we play this down a bit so she can focus on her run? Not let our guard down. Just not make a big deal of it with her."

Walt ground his teeth for a moment but then nodded. "I'm glad to oblige, and I'm sure everyone else agrees. But I need to be assured that she's taking the threat seriously."

"Don't worry," Braden said. "She is, and so am I."

TEN

"Do you always get VIP treatment like this at events?" Braden asked in the arena barn as Tessa braided Copper's mane. There weren't enough stalls for every contestant, so most of them kept their horses tied to their trailers.

"I shouldn't have to tell you about the perks of being a celebrity." She turned to smile at him. "Granted I'm only a local celebrity, and this is only a stall, but you get what I mean."

He did indeed, and he wanted to play along with her good humor and say something funny, but he couldn't relax. How could he when Ingram might be after her? If the creep hurt his own grandmother, what might he do to Tessa?

"It's time, fella," she said to Copper.

Braden wished he could let her go without reminding her of the danger before her run, but he couldn't. "Remember, once you finish your run, head straight back here to minimize the threat to your life."

Her smile evaporated. "I got it."

He hated seeing her upset and the desire to kiss her cheek and tell her everything would be okay was nearly overwhelming. Not a good idea for so many reasons, but most important, kissing her now was guaranteed to distract her even further—the last thing she needed with the competition and a felon gunning for her.

He stepped aside, and they exited the deserted barn. Tessa was the last rider of the evening. Many contestants, and even some fans, had already left for the night, making it easier to scan the area for Ingram and Falby.

Braden nodded at the volunteer guarding the gate to the barn area. He was dressed in the usual cowboy fare and had a tough demeanor. Not that people would likely challenge him to access the barn without permission, but Braden was glad to know this guy manned the gate.

As they crossed the street, and then the large parking lot, Braden searched between trucks and trailers. Through groups of contestants sitting by campers. Through groups of fans chattering excitedly as they collected autographs.

A wave of melancholy hit Braden. He could easily get caught up in the rodeo excitement if he didn't have Tessa to protect, but she was his top priority. He didn't relax, not even when they safely reached the participant entrance guarded by two volunteers. They wished her well and she mounted Copper. She urged him forward to a side chute next to the alleyway where two racers waited ahead of Tessa. She came to a stop behind them and sat back in her saddle. The announcer's voice echoed through the night, his tone fevered as he tried to excite the crowd.

Braden always loved it in the arena when the crowd was with him, but right now their cheers might cover threats he needed to hear, and he didn't like it. At all. Thankfully, he'd gotten permission to at least escort Tessa inside the arena and watch from a nearby viewing area.

The first racer took off, her horse's hooves kicking up the soil. Until this moment, he hadn't thought about Tessa's run from the racing point of view. While his top priority was her safety, he still wanted her to take home the championship buckle again this year, and he worried that all of his warnings had made her timid.

He tugged on her hand to encourage her to bend down close enough to hear him above the excited crowd. "You've got this, you know. I've seen you ride, and you're one of the best."

"Thank you," she smiled, but it suddenly disappeared. "I'm not being foolish, am I? Riding with someone out there wanting to do me in, I mean. Once I hit the arena, no one can protect me. Not you. Not dad. No one."

As the other racer took off, Braden squeezed her hand. "Trust me. If I thought the danger was too great, I wouldn't have let you out of the barn. Just remember to meet me back here afterward and you'll be fine. Now concentrate on the run and bring home the championship one more time."

The announcer called her name, and she moved Copper into the alleyway. He saw her slide her hands down her reins to get them in position. He stepped to the viewing area, and when she shot into the arena, his heart clutched. She was exposed. Wide-open to danger, and he wouldn't be able to help her should a problem arise.

Tessa flew toward the first barrel. She was in the zone and nothing else mattered. Not the crowd. Not the world. Just Copper and her run.

She circled it, the wind blowing in her face. She kicked Copper faster toward the second barrel. Moved at top speed. Circled around. Went for the third one. Finished the cloverleaf pattern. Head forward, she raced toward the electric eye that would stop the clock, then booked it out of the arena.

The crowd was on their feet cheering. It was a good run. A great one, actually. She just knew it. Adrenaline raced through her veins, and she turned back to see her time. 13.88 seconds.

Yes! Nearly her record time, and it put her at the top of the leaderboard.

The crowd chanted her name.

"C'mon back and take a bow, Tessa," the announcer called out.

As the last contestant of the night, she didn't need to worry about other horses in the alleyway, so she turned and trotted into the arena. Thunderous applause broke out. She stood in her stirrups, took off her hat and bowed. The audience went wild. What a blessing to do so well in the first run of three in her final competition.

She heard someone shouting her name. Braden. She'd let the adrenaline take over and had forgotten her promise to depart right away. Embarrassed, she dropped into the saddle and exited the arena.

"What in the world were you thinking going back in there?" Braden grabbed Copper's reins as if he planned to tow him to the barn.

Braden was fortunate Copper was so friendly or Copper could have chomped on Braden's hand. And he was fortunate that she didn't snap back at him. She'd simply forgotten. She shouldn't have, but she'd gotten caught up in the moment.

She dismounted. "I know you want me to race to the barn, but Copper needs to cool down, and he chooses to jig and dance with me in the saddle, so I'll walk."

She slightly loosened the cinch and started Copper moving toward the barn. She didn't take her safety for granted and kept searching the area as she moved. When they passed the security volunteer at the gate, she relaxed for the remaining walk to the barn. She put Copper in the stall to finish removing his tack.

Braden stepped close to her, his hands fisted on his waist. "That was completely irresponsible."

She arched a brow and looked at him. "I was wrong for letting the adrenaline get to me and forgetting. I'm sorry for that. Really, I am. But it's done and we should move on."

"Done?" His voice skyrocketed. "Done? I won't have you blowing this off. If you want to run again, you need to promise that you won't forget any instructions I've given you."

"Won't have me? If I want to run again?" she snapped at him "You're not in charge of me, Braden. I listened to your advice because it was good advice. But I'm not going to be bossed around when I have the skills to make a sound decision about my safety."

He stepped even closer. "I'm responsible for you. I promised your dad. Your family. I won't let them down. Let *you* down. So you need to do exactly as I say."

"I made a mistake."

"That's no excuse," he ground out between clenched teeth. "You could have died."

He was exaggerating now. Sure, there was a greater chance that someone could have hurt her when she was out in the arena with no protection—but it was hardly likely, or her family wouldn't have let her compete in the first place. And anyway, nothing happened! She couldn't believe he refused to accept that she'd made a mistake.

Reminded her of her brothers. Her dad. Always thinking they could tell her what to do. Refusing to accept her competence. Her anger bubbled up until she felt like she might choke from it. She needed air. She closed the stall door and stomped out of the barn. She'd seen her family in the arena, and she'd find them. She'd be safe with them, and not have to put up with Braden telling her what to do.

She moved quickly, her anger fueling her steps, but she made sure to be aware of her surroundings. She charged around the corner and heard Braden behind her. Fine, but she wasn't going to slow down for him.

And she'd thought she was starting to fall for him. Ha! Fall for someone so controlling? No way. Imagine a lifetime of that behavior. She'd be tired of it in a day, much less until death do us part. She picked up speed.

She wouldn't slow down for anything.

What about Copper?

Her footsteps faltered. She'd been so mad she'd ignored her responsibility to her horse. Left him to fend for himself after he'd given her the ride of her life. She'd left her best friend behind when he needed her care. Unacceptable. She spun and faced Braden.

"I have to tend to Copper." She pushed past him. She heard his booted footfalls as he came after her. Even with her anger, he was there, trying to protect her. He only wanted what was best for her. Same with her dad and brothers. Didn't mean it didn't still irritate her, but she knew she'd overreacted. Let her temper get to her.

"It's Braden Hayes," a young woman called out, and Tessa heard the resulting giggles of the other women in the group. "Can we get your autograph, Braden?"

Tessa didn't wait around to see the swooning females. She might be cross with him, but she didn't like the thought of these women swarming around him. Reminded her too much of Jason. She was nearly to the barn, and once there, she'd be fine on her own. She rounded the corner to her stall entrance. Lights that were burning bright only a moment ago were now out, and the darkness had her feet faltering. They'd recently installed motion-sensor lights at the barn to save money. They should have come on.

"Tessa, wait up," Braden yelled, but he needn't have, as her gut told her something was wrong.

She spun to leave.

She hurried back in the direction she'd come, but an arm shot out from the dark and around her neck. A man jerked her back against his body. She opened her mouth to scream, but the arm cut off her oxygen and only a pitiful whimper escaped.

ELEVEN

"Tessa?" Braden called again, his gut tightening when she didn't answer. He pushed past the women and heard them complain, but getting to Tessa was all he could think about. He rounded the corner. Saw the barn lights extinguished. Saw two people struggling in the moonlight.

Tessa. A man with his arm around her neck was dragging her backward.

"Freeze! Police!" Braden shouted and shot forward.

Tessa lifted her arm. Elbowed the man in the gut. Reached up and grabbed his hair.

"Ugh," he grunted and released her. He spun and bolted into the shadows.

Braden wanted to chase after the attacker, but tending to Tessa was more important. He raced to her side. "Are you okay?"

"Fine." She rubbed her neck, but her hand was trembling.

"C'mon." He took her by the arm to lower her

onto a wooden crate by the building while pulling out his phone. He dialed her father and reported the incident to ask for backup and for someone to go after her attacker.

When Braden finished his call, he squatted in front of her. Her eyes were wild—terrified—her gaze darting around. Her breathing was labored, and he feared she would hyperventilate.

"Take deep breaths, darlin'. Big deep breaths." He took a few himself to demonstrate, but also to let go of his own anxiety. They stayed that way for how long he didn't know, but he saw her fear finally abate and the knot in his gut loosened.

"I'm sorry," he said. "This's all my fault. I over-reacted, and even after you apologized, I kept at you. If I hadn't, you might not have taken off just now." He moved closer, met her gaze and held it. "It's just…when I saw you in the arena, not moving, a potential target, I couldn't breathe. Couldn't think. So when I got your attention and could talk to you, all I could think to do was make you promise it would never happen again, and I became too demanding."

"No, wait." She held up a hand. "You didn't do anything wrong. It was me. I shouldn't have let my temper get the best of me and run off. I appreciate your help. You. I appreciate you." Her gaze darkened, that of a woman interested in a man, and he so reveled to see it that he had to touch her.

He rested his forehead on hers. "Why don't we agree we both were at fault?"

"And promise not to let it happen again," she whispered, her breath soft on his face.

He loved being so close to her, but he wanted more. He wanted to kiss her. To taste her lips and soak in the connection he'd never felt in his life. He lifted his head. Kept hold of her gaze. Thought to ask before kissing her, but couldn't even wait the amount of time it would take.

He lowered his head. Pressed his lips against hers. Warm, soft, yielding, she responded. Eager and willing. Like she'd found something she'd long been searching for. He sure had.

He deepened the kiss. She slid a hand behind his neck and pulled him closer. He couldn't believe the emotions crashing through his body, and he lost all track of time. Place. Everything but Tessa.

"Tessa! Girl, where are you?" The sheriff's worried voice broke through Braden's fog, and he jerked his head away.

He continued to look at Tessa, her gaze filling with regret, perhaps from the kiss ending so abruptly. She took a long breath, then kissed the tip of his nose before turning her head.

"Here, Dad," she shouted. "I'm here."

Walt barreled around the corner, turned back and yelled, "You girls go on home now. No autographs to be had here. And someone get these lights on." He hurried to Tessa. "Are you all right?"

"I'm fine. Just a few bruises."

Braden wasn't surprised when she tugged her shirt collar closed. He suspected she didn't want her dad to see the extent of her bruises when the lights came on.

He suddenly spun on Braden. "How could you let this happen?"

"I wish I could say I didn't, but—"

"It was my fault," Tessa interrupted. "I took off, and Braden got waylaid by some fans. I could have stopped to wait for him, but I didn't."

"That's not the whole—"

"But it's all fine." Tessa held up her hand and stood. "I jerked some hair out of his head. We should get the strands in an evidence bag so we can process for DNA. I have them in my truck. I'll secure this, then tend to Copper."

"I'll get someone else to take care of Copper." Walt faced Braden. "I'd like to escort Tessa to her truck myself, but I have to direct my deputies in a manhunt. So I need to count on you. If she takes off on you again, hog-tie her and toss her in the truck."

"Dad!" Tessa's eyes widened.

"Peanut, if that's what it takes to keep you safe, then that's what Braden is authorized to do."

Braden expected her to argue about his demands or even say she needed to collect additional evidence, but she headed for the parking lot.

"Listen to Braden," Walt called after her. "And stay close to him."

"I will, Dad. I promise."

Braden didn't like the defeated bent to her tone, but he did like that she'd promised to listen and stay close, as he knew her attacker hadn't given up. He would come back again. The only questions were when and where.

Tessa did just as she'd promised. She stuck close to Braden. Probably too close for a deputy who should stand on her own two feet. But honestly, fear didn't have her clinging to him. Sure, fear lingered, but the emotions tumbling through her from kissing him were what had her glued to his side.

She'd never felt anything like it. Not the kiss—but the warm, exhilarating feeling taking over her heart afterward that she'd never experienced with any other guy. Not even with Jason. It was probably the fear and adrenaline all mixing together with Braden's tenderness that caused the emotions, but she wanted more of that sensation. Much more.

Near the arena, Braden opened her truck door. "You should sit. I'll get the bag."

She thought to argue, but her muscles were still wobbly, so she plopped down on the seat and let her legs dangle out the door while he retrieved the bags. He came back around the truck and opened one. She carefully released the captured hair inside.

The bright arena lights revealed the good news that she'd gotten a few roots with the hairs, further ensuring the retrieval of DNA. "I need to get right to preparing the samples for the state lab."

"I take it you don't have the equipment to run DNA here."

She started to shake her head but stopped when the pain from her neck grew intense. "I'm sure Dad will try to get this bumped up the list, and we won't have to wait long for the results."

Braden nodded, but his attention shifted to a pair of women laughing near the arena. Tessa followed his gaze to Felicia Peters and a woman Tessa didn't recognize. Felicia suddenly turned to look at Tessa, a triumphant gleam in her eyes. She couldn't be feeling superior over her first run. Not with Tessa beating her time. So what was the gleam about?

"You know them?" Braden asked.

"The blonde is Felicia Peters." Tessa kept her focus on the woman. "Something about the way she's looking right now is rubbing me the wrong way. She wouldn't be feeling high and mighty over her run, that's for sure. So maybe she had something to do with the attack. Or at the very least, she knew about it." Tessa pushed to her feet. "I aim to go over there and ask her."

Braden planted his feet and blocked her way. "Hold on there. Let's calm down and think this through."

She would have skirted around him, but she'd just promised to listen to him, so she remained put and took a few calming breaths.

"With the way she dislikes you, she's not likely to give you a straight answer. Why don't you let me question her alone?" Braden gestured at Kendall, who was approaching them. "You can sit tight with your sister, and I'll do my best to get Felicia to talk."

Tessa took a breath and nodded, but her body still vibrated with the urge to confront Felicia. Sure, Tessa had no concrete reason to think the woman was involved, but Tessa needed to feel like she was doing something to find the man who'd just attacked her.

"You okay, sis?" Kendall asked, her gaze searching Tessa from head to toe.

Tessa buttoned her collar and nodded.

Braden faced Kendall. "Mind hanging with Tessa while I go talk to Felicia?"

"Go," Kendall said, but her attention remained on Tessa.

Braden walked away, and Tessa tracked his long-legged stride.

"So," Kendall said. "What are you hiding under the collar?"

"I haven't looked, but the guy caught me around the neck and choked me." She swung her gaze to her sister. "It hurts like crazy, so I assume there are bruises, and I don't want Dad to see them. Promise me you won't say anything."

"He should know about it."

"What good would it serve other than for him to get even more protective?"

"Maybe that's what you need."

"Braden's protective enough." *If I learn to keep my cool and listen to him.* "I can't deal with Dad going overboard, too."

Kendall's gaze snapped back to Braden. "He's quite the flirt, isn't he?"

Tessa swiveled to watch him. He was leaning against the building, his posture relaxed, a smile on his face. His attention was riveted to Felicia, and she was smiling up at him. Tessa knew how Felicia was feeling. She was putty in Braden's hands, willing to do just about anything to keep that mesmerizing smile fixed on her.

He came to his full height and planted his legs wide, looking like the fierce defender Tessa knew him to be. He placed a hand on Felicia's shoulder, and she seemed like she might melt. Tessa's stomach tightened, and she felt as if she was going to be sick.

Had she gone beyond physical attraction with Braden to caring about him? Sure, she knew he held a special place in her heart for his rescues, but this feeling had nothing to do with that. She didn't want to care about him in a romantic sense. Care about any man that way. It only led to heartache.

Do you really want to spend your life alone? The thought hit her upside the head, and she had to ponder it. Maybe she should pray about it. She hadn't, after all. At least, not really. She'd decided the night she caught Jason cheating on her that love was out of the question in her future and hadn't even consulted God. But that had been wrong. So wrong, and she should have taken it to God in prayer.

But even if she did consult God, even if she determined this was what He wanted for her, she could still be terribly hurt again. Was she willing to risk that?

"Braden kind of reminds me of Jason," Kendall said.

"You think?" She watched him more carefully and couldn't tell if he was putting on an act or if the flirtation was real. Either way, it served as a good reminder. She couldn't see how his seeming interest in Felicia could be real after the kiss they'd shared, but then it might not have meant as much to Braden.

Did it matter, anyway? She might have kissed him, but she was still a long way from trusting a man with her heart again.

TWELVE

Braden's anger had fired the minute he'd caught a look at the deep purple bruises on Tessa's neck during an early morning jog they'd taken before breakfast. He'd suggested she see a doctor, but she'd told him to leave it alone. So he had. Now, as they sat down to breakfast, he could see only a tiny fraction of the bruises, and he suspected she'd covered them up with makeup.

She leaned forward to grab the orange juice pitcher and grimaced. So they were painful, too. Made him even madder. He wanted to find a windowless room with impenetrable walls and put her inside until they arrested her attacker, but he knew she'd have none of it. And he respected her enough to allow her to move about with proper backup. As long as she made good on her promise and listened.

"What's this I hear about you having a bull riding clinic today, Braden?" Jed asked.

Braden looked at Jed. "It's an introductory lesson for local teens interested in the sport."

"Are you going to be riding a bull?" Winnie asked.

Braden nodded.

"But that's dangerous, and you're out of practice," Tessa protested.

"I appreciate your concern, but I can handle it."

She frowned, and if he didn't know better, he'd think she was worried for him. Not just for his safety as a fellow human being, but because she might be having some of the same overwhelming feelings he'd been experiencing since last night's kiss.

"And what about Tessa?" Betty's worried gaze landed on Tessa. "Will she be somewhere safe while you do this clinic?"

"Kendall and I'll be in the press box taking Perry Richter's prints," Tessa said.

"Perry?" Betty clutched her chest. "Surely, you don't think he's in on this."

Tessa shook her head. "Since he handles the lock at the arena, we want his prints so if they're on the lock we can eliminate them."

"Ah, I see."

Jed sat forward and rested his hands on the table. "The clinic sounds interesting. Mind if I sit in?"

"I don't mind at all," Braden replied. "In fact,

you can keep an eye out for Falby's pink vest, and if he's wearing it, give it a good once-over to look for any damage."

"Happy to help." A wide grin spread across Jed's face.

Betty patted his hand. "You don't know how happy you've made this retired lawman."

The grin widened even more, and Braden suddenly wondered what his own grandparents were like. He hoped if he ever saw them again that they turned out to be decent folks.

"FYI, I heard back from Ernie Winston." Matt picked up his empty plate and got to his feet. "He has a ranch hand who wears pink gloves, but no one who wears a pink vest. She claims she didn't snag a glove. I'll have a deputy in Ernie's part of the state confirm his story."

"Then hopefully Falby will show up today," Braden said.

Matt passed Kendall as she entered the dining room, carrying a thick folder.

She stopped to stare at the file, before tossing it onto the table next to Tessa. "Ingram's file. Thought you'd want to read through it before heading out to interview him."

"I'll be interviewing him as soon as he's found." Tessa lifted her chin and stared at her brother as if she thought he'd challenge her decision to interview Ingram.

"Just let me know what you learn once you *do* connect with him." Matt departed and Braden caught a quick shake of Walt's head. The sheriff didn't like something about Matt's decision, but he didn't put voice to it.

"Once I locate Ingram, I'll text you," Kendall said.

"The sooner, the better." Though it went without saying, Braden had felt compelled to add it.

"Can you stay for breakfast?" Winnie asked her daughter.

Kendall shook her head. "I'm on duty in fifteen minutes, but I can never resist one of Nana's muffins to go."

Braden could totally understand the temptation, as he'd already consumed two of them. "With Betty's amazing baking, I don't know how you all aren't seriously overweight."

"Gym," Kendall and Tessa replied at the same time.

"A place I can tell you're no stranger to," Betty said, and when his mouth fell open in surprise, she winked. "I might be old, but I'm not blind."

Heat raced up Braden's neck. He rarely blushed, and he shot a look at Tessa to see her reaction. She frowned. She'd been somewhat terse with him after he'd talked to Felicia last night, but he hadn't done anything wrong, so he didn't think that was the reason for her mood. Maybe her current attitude had nothing to do with the conversation, and she was regretting the kiss. Adrenaline and feeling safe after her attacker vanished could have swept her up and she'd kissed him for those reasons alone. He didn't much like the idea and wanted to think the way she'd responded proved she cared about him, but he could see how the adrenaline could have gotten to her.

She stood and picked up the folder. "I'm gonna get started on reviewing this."

She left the room without inviting Braden to join her, but he didn't need an invite. He would get a look inside that file, too.

"Excuse me," he said and collected his and Tessa's dirty plates.

"Thank you," Winnie said. "Tessa has a lot on her mind, or I'd call her out on leaving her plate behind."

"I don't mind clearing it for her."

Winnie smiled up at him. "You're a good man, Braden, and we're fortunate to have met you."

Winnie's words wrapped him in warmth as he took the plates to the kitchen. He tried to shrug the feeling off. He was a grown man, and here he was letting a simple compliment puff up his ego. But he'd never gotten such kind words from his own parents, and it meant a lot to hear it from Winnie. Meant too much, he was beginning to think.

He found Tessa in her father's office, sitting behind a large mahogany desk. She glanced up for just a moment and turned back to the folder lying open in front of her. He didn't wait for an invitation but went to stand behind her. She scooted closer to the desk and that made him mad.

"I'm not going to try to kiss you again," he said. "So you don't have to worry."

She looked up at him. "So you know it was a mistake, too."

He didn't, but at her convincing tone, he nodded and made sure his disappointment didn't show on his face. He looked at the file and Ingram's picture. His jet-black hair was nothing like the hair sample Tessa had recovered last night.

"Hair color's wrong," Braden said.

"Black isn't Ingram's natural color. He was into the Goth look back then. But I have no idea if he still is now."

"So what have you found?"

"I've scanned his prison record." She tapped the page. "He didn't manage to get parole, so he served his complete sentence."

Braden looked at the page and saw two altercations with other prisoners. No wonder the parole board considered him too dangerous to release. "It looks like he still believes in using violence."

She nodded.

"What kind of guy beats his own grandmother,

anyway? Can you imagine one of your brothers beating up Betty? It's utterly unfathomable."

"I wondered the same thing. When the call first came in, I thought maybe his grandmother was abusive, and he simply struck back, but as I talked to her, I learned she's a sweet lady." Tessa flipped the next page in the file.

Braden recognized it as the visitor log from Ingram's prison stay. "His grandmother and father both visited on a regular basis."

"Could mean when he got out that they let him come home. Maybe we shouldn't wait until Kendall locates him, just head out there now."

"I'd rather not tip our hat if he's not there. His dad or grandmother could warn him, and he might go into hiding. Besides, with Douglas Peters's hair color matching the evidence sample, I'd rather follow up with him." Braden had learned nothing from Felicia last night, but he did catch a look at her brother again, and his hair color looked like it could be a match for the sample in Tessa's evidence bag.

She swiveled. "Ingram's hair could be the same color, too. We just don't know."

"But we *do* know Douglas seems to be a match."

"And he has the right build for the guy who attacked me," Tessa added. "Last I remember of Ingram, he was of average build. The guy last night was burly."

"So if we haven't heard from Kendall by the time we finish going through this file, we'll head out to the Peters' ranch."

"Okay." She gestured at a side chair. "But I can't concentrate with you hanging over me, so take a seat."

He did, but instead of sitting to the side where he couldn't see the file, he scooted around the corner of the desk next to her. His leg bumped hers, and she jerked it away.

Wow. The kiss was totally freaking her out. Freaked him out, too, but in a much different way. In fact, everything around her was bothering him. Her family. Their closeness. His longing to be a part of something like this family team. And they were a team. All working together for the good of one of their members. Sort of like his law enforcement family, but more. So much more.

On Douglas's doorstep, Tessa rang the doorbell. "We need to be ready for him to run again."

Braden's eyebrow quirked up. "You think he will?"

"Wouldn't put it past him." She took a strong stance and was glad when Braden followed suit.

Douglas opened the door, the frown Tessa always associated with him plastered on his face. "Felicia's not here, if you've come to gloat over your first-place status."

"We're not here for Felicia, we're here for you." Tessa worked hard not to snap at him and put up his guard.

"Me? I told you everything I know about the bull."

"I'm sure you heard about my attack last night."

"Yeah, I heard. So what?" He crossed his arms. She eyed him.

"Wait, you can't be thinking I had something to do with it." His face paled. "That's just ludicrous."

"Where were you last night?" she asked.

"At the rodeo with everyone else in town. I saw your run. Saw you head back into the arena afterward all full of yourself. I was in the stands—nowhere near you."

"You could simply have heard about that from your sister," Braden pointed out. "Is there anyone who can confirm you were in the arena at the time of the attack?"

Douglas shrugged. "Someone must have seen me climbing up to the press box, but I didn't recognize anyone sitting in the nosebleed section."

"As a volunteer you get front row seats," Tessa said. "Why were you way up there?"

"Because," he snarled at her. "I always take my binoculars to make sure the clock starts and stops the second Felicia passes the electric eye.

Your run, too. Wouldn't put it past you McKades to rig it."

Tessa wanted to snap at him but held her tongue. After all, what was the point in protesting? He was clearly irrational. "We'd like to take a DNA sample."

"DNA! No. No way. Not without talking to my lawyer."

"If what you're saying is true," Braden said, "the sample could help clear your name of further allegations."

"I said no."

There had to be a reason he was being so adamant, but Tessa couldn't think of even one other than that he was guilty of something else. For now, she'd move them along. "Do you know Cliff Falby?"

"We were in the same class at school."

"Talk to him lately?"

"No." She stared into his eyes and saw no hint of guile.

He may have bad-mouthed her in the bar. Given away information and changed the check-in schedule on the hope that it would mess things up for her, but none of it was a criminal offence unless they could prove he knew what the outcome would be. Still, she wanted him to be guilty—to confess to the attacks—because then these threats to her life would end.

Tessa widened her stance and met his gaze. "You know what will happen if I find out you're lying to us."

"Yeah, more police brutality," he sneered.

Braden took a step toward Douglas, and he backed into his house and closed the door.

"So much for that," Tessa said. "We can't compel him to give us his DNA without a warrant, and we don't have enough probable cause to get that."

"It seems like you're thinking he could have teamed up with Falby."

"Honestly, I just threw it out there to see how Douglas would react, but he either hid it well or they aren't in cahoots."

"I concur."

They started toward the truck, and her phone rang with Kendall's special ringtone. Tessa quickly answered.

"Ingram is living at the family ranch," Kendall said. "In fact, I know he's there right now, so you might want to hightail it over there."

THIRTEEN

Braden didn't think Ingram's family ranch could be more in direct contrast to Serenity Ranch. Lush grass and shrubbery circled the house, and someone had recently painted the fence surrounding big corrals a brilliant white.

Braden parked by the two-story colonial-style home, which was also freshly painted a crisp white with black shutters. "Looks like the Ingrams have some money."

Tessa nodded. "They made it in oil. Spoiled Junior something awful. He was always trying to find a few kicks and kept getting into trouble. Millard Senior used his connections to keep Junior out of jail until I arrested him for hitting his grandmother."

"Glad to hear the DA drew the line there." Braden removed his keys. "Why didn't you mention Junior's priors?"

"I figured the lesser charges weren't relevant."

"Maybe they are and Senior is involved in

this. You know, paying you back for putting his kid away."

She shook her head. "At least, I don't see it. Senior is a decent kind of guy. Law-abiding. His only weakness is turning a blind eye to his son. Besides, if he wanted to pay me back, I don't think he'd wait until Junior got out."

"Good point." Braden climbed out. At the front door, he waited for Tessa to say she was taking charge, but for some reason she didn't mention it and rang the bell.

Junior himself answered the door. He wore holey jeans that hung low on his hips, a Grateful Dead T-shirt, and his hair was black as midnight. Still, they had no way of knowing how long it had been that way. He could have dyed it that morning. And he looked pretty buff. He could have bulked up in prison, lifting weights to pass the time.

"You," he spit out between clenched teeth as his fiery-mad gaze latched on to Tessa. "What do you want?"

Braden was impressed that she didn't back down or even flinch, but he wasn't going to let the guy's threatening attitude go without moving closer to her.

"I need to know where you were last night around eight thirty," she said matter-of-factly, as if the guy hadn't just snapped at her.

"At the rodeo."

"Can anyone vouch for you?"

"I was with a few buds." His gaze remained glued to her. "Seems like you think I did something, but I was in the stands until the closing event. I can give you a play-by-play of the action if that will help."

"That information's easy enough to come by," Braden said.

His gaze shot to Braden as fast as a bull whipping his body around. "And you are?"

"Braden Hayes. Austin homicide detective." Braden wished he had his badge to display for added emphasis, but he didn't carry his credentials off duty.

"Wow. Austin cops are after me now, too." Ingram smirked. "What kind of lies have you spread about me this time, McKade?"

"Why would your fingerprints be on the padlock for the arena gate?" she asked, ignoring his taunting like any good deputy would.

He jutted out his jaw. "I have no idea."

"Your body language tells me otherwise." She moved closer to him and pinned him with her gaze. "You want to head into the office to talk about this?"

"Nothing to talk about." He crossed his arms, revealing a tattoo of a clock without hands on his wrist. Braden had seen similar prison tattoos that represented doing time.

"Your prints are on the gate padlock," Tessa said. "It's an indisputable fact. Tell us how they got there, or I'm taking you in."

He frowned, but his expression had lost some bravado. "Hypothetically speaking, a guy might want to party with his buds on the first Saturday night he finally gets out of prison. And a closed arena might be a good place to party. So he might try the lock, and when he can't get it open, maybe he hops the fence with his buds."

"And could this hypothetical guy produce the name of his buddies for an alibi?" Braden asked, playing along, though he'd rather grab the guy by his T-shirt and threaten him if he didn't give them the information they sought.

"Hypothetically, he might have been with Iggy and Oden Williams."

Tessa snorted. "That's a law-abiding pair to vouch for you."

He crossed his arms. "I served my full sentence. No parole means no probation for me. So you can't tell me who to hang with."

"And where were you on Wednesday morning around seven?" she asked.

His eyebrow rose. "Here. In bed, sleeping off the night before. My dad and grandmother will be glad to confirm that for you."

"I'll just bet they will," Tessa muttered.

"Like you should be the one with an attitude," he snapped. "I'm the one who went away for a crime I didn't commit. Thanks to you. And I'll never forget that." He raised a finger as if he planned to poke her in the chest.

Braden shot out a hand and deflected it. His gut churned with anger over the creep trying to touch Tessa. He wanted to take the man's finger and twist, but Ingram was the kind of guy who would claim police brutality. Braden wasn't that kind of officer, plus he wouldn't give him the opportunity. Not when the guy's hateful attitude toward Tessa made him a strong contender for the creep trying to end her life, and giving him a viable complaint against them could jeopardize getting any future arrest to stick.

At the arena, Tessa watched Braden head down the steps to the field from the press box, leaving her standing at the window with Kendall at her side.

"I have to admit I have a soft spot for cowboys in chaps and spurs," Kendall said.

Braden turned back to look up at them and Tessa's heart clutched. She didn't care about the chaps or the spurs. Not at all, but the stubble he was allowing to grow along with his hat pulled low made him look darkly dangerous standing there.

"Looks like you do, too," Kendall said. "Or is it just *this* cowboy?"

Tessa snapped her gaze away but said nothing.

"You can admit it, you know."

"Right. Sure. Even if I did have feelings for him, after you said he reminded you of Jason last night, I'm not about to act on them."

"I shouldn't have said that."

"Why not? You thought it."

"Yeah, but he's not really like Jason where it counts. Sure, he might flirt like him, but there's depth to Braden. You have to be seeing that."

Tessa had noticed. Boy, how she'd noticed. She was growing more and more impressed with him. With everything he'd accomplished since his difficult childhood. With his manners and respectful behavior, and with his dedication to keeping her safe.

She was really starting to enjoy having him around. Enjoy having him as her sidekick while she investigated. Enjoy sharing things with a man, something she was beginning to think she'd like more of.

Imagine that. Her. A non-people person. Someone who, after her one long-term relationship had left her reeling, had been happy to hole up in her forensic cave. Wanting something more now. Not like it mattered. Even if Braden returned her feelings, he didn't live in Lost Creek, and she'd never leave her family.

What about Dad's offer? Might Braden be willing to give up his life in Austin and make the move out to the country?

"Mom and Nana can't quit talking about how wonderful he is, and that says a lot," Kendall continued.

"They liked Jason, too."

"Um, actually…they didn't."

Tessa swiveled to face her sister. "What? Why didn't they say anything?"

"They knew you'd eventually see through him and it would fizzle out, and there was no point in mentioning it after you'd broken up."

Tessa sighed. "It's so much easier to be single."

"But not nearly as fun." Kendall winked.

"Says someone who has been perpetually single."

Kendall's good humor evaporated from her face.

"Sorry, sis, that was mean."

"But true," Kendall said. "I don't have time. I need to have proved myself by the time Dad retires and Matt runs for sheriff so I can get Matt's detective position."

"You will, and if you don't, the other spot will be opening up in a year or so."

"So what?" She sighed. "You know Dad can't

show us any favoritism, so we have to be far better at our jobs than anyone else to move up the ladder."

"True," Tessa said. She was about to continue, but a commotion on the field took her attention.

A black-and-white bull stood in the chute, and Braden was climbing on the animal's back.

"Is that King Slammer?" Kendall asked.

"Looks like him. I know that Braden picked the bull and had to get the owner's approval, but he never mentioned who he chose."

"If it is, maybe he's avenging your honor with the bull." Kendall laughed.

Tessa chuckled, too, but it would be just like the man she was coming to know to do something like that. He started rubbing the bull rope—the one that circled around the bull and the rider held on to—with his gloved hand to warm up the rosin he'd applied earlier. This would make the rope sticky to prevent his hand from popping out of the rope looped around his hand during the ride.

Tessa had seen this chute procedure tons of times. Seen Braden do it and ride many times, too, but she'd never gotten this queasy feeling in the pit of her stomach before. She moved closer to the window. Placed a hand against the ledge to steady herself as her legs suddenly felt like they were made of jelly.

"You *do* care about him," Kendall said.

Tessa spun. "Why do you say that?"

"The look on your face. Half of you is proud of and impressed with him. The other half, scared to death for him."

Tessa shook her head. "I guess if you got all that from one look, you're going to make a mighty fine detective."

Tessa heard the gate clang open and spun to watch the bull bolt into the arena. Braden had his arm up in a perfect L shape. The bull bucked. Twisted. Jumped. The teens in the stand were on their feet cheering.

"You got this, Braden," she said, without thinking.

He was jarred back and forth, his arm flailing up and down. His hat flew off, but he hung on, making it all look so easy. Still, it seemed like an eternity passed before the eight-second timer buzzed, and he flipped his leg over the bull's head to slip off and landed on his feet. Two bullfighters dressed in bright T-shirts shooed the bull away from Braden and into the chute.

He grabbed his hat from the dirt, and as he dusted it off against his chaps, he looked up at the press box and made eye contact. Her heart skipped a beat, and she had to admit she was so thankful that he no longer rode bulls on a regular basis. Her heart could never take the strain.

* * *

Braden got the truck on the road to Iggy and Oden Williams's apartment to confirm Ingram's alibi, but Braden's mind drifted back to the arena. Falby had shown up, his trademark pink vest fully intact. With the price of a custom bull riding vest, and Falby not seeming to have much money, Braden figured the guy didn't own a second one, but Braden couldn't prove that.

He was disappointed they hadn't confirmed Falby's involvement, but at the same time, Braden was too pumped about the ride to feel down about it. Man, it'd been a blast. Almost made him want to come out of retirement. Tomorrow morning would be another story. Every muscle in his body would ache, and he'd pay for those eight seconds of adrenaline.

But still, what a rush. And he'd stayed on. Even better.

Tessa swiveled to face him. "You're awfully quiet."

"I'm reliving the ride." He grinned at her. "Did you happen to notice I chose King Slammer? Thought I ought to show the guy he can't go running around and threatening someone I care about."

She frowned.

"What's wrong?" he asked, wondering if she had a problem hearing that he cared about her.

"I didn't like seeing you on the bull."

"Hey, it was a perfect ride. What's not to like?" He grinned.

She didn't even crack a smile. "I don't know. You possibly being hurled to the ground. The bull stomping on you. Goring you. You name it, and it could go wrong." She sighed.

"I guess it was pretty irresponsible of me when I promised to keep an eye on you."

"No… I mean…that's not it."

"Then what?"

"You could have been hurt. Seriously hurt."

"I lived with that threat for years, and it's no big deal."

"It is to me." She crossed her arms and faced the door.

He didn't know what to make of her comment. Did she honestly care about him as more than her bodyguard, or would she be this concerned for any bull rider? Couldn't be the last, as she participated in a dangerous sport herself, and it would have been odd if she reacted this way for just anyone.

He wanted to ask, but he wouldn't. It didn't matter if she cared about him. Despite any growing feelings, he would make sure to keep things platonic between them, as he still wasn't relationship material. He needed to change the topic back to business. "Tell me about the Williams brothers."

She continued to stare out the window. "They're twins in their midtwenties. Druggies who can't seem to stay out of trouble."

"So they'll say whatever Ingram wants them to say."

"Likely, but we still have to question them."

"Hopefully, if they lie, we can catch them in it."

"Hopefully," she said, her tone distant as if she didn't want to talk.

He got the hint and kept his trap shut as he navigated through town to a rundown apartment building on the outskirts. Two stories tall, it had faded paint, rusted railings and trash in the parking lot.

Braden parked outside the twins' apartment on the first floor. "Nice place."

"Isn't it? You can rent by the day here, and it's a known drug den."

Braden didn't like Tessa even getting out of the truck in this neighborhood, but she was a deputy after all and had likely responded to places like this while on patrol.

At the door, they knocked and then she looked at him and reached up to adjust his hair. He gaped at her in surprise.

"Hat hair," she said and jerked her hand away as if she suddenly realized what she had done.

"Thanks, then."

She suddenly looked like she realized her action had been extremely personal, and she blushed. He loved her innocence mixed with the tough deputy vibe she usually displayed.

The door opened and a skinny man with stringy blond hair and a vacant stare peered at them. His eyes were bloodshot, his pupils large. Perhaps they'd had good timing and the brothers were stoned and would willingly share the information they needed.

Tessa displayed her credentials. "Are you Iggy or Oden?"

"Iggy," he said.

"May we come in?"

He stepped back, nearly stumbling, and they entered a small box of a room that smelled like a cross between dirty gym socks and marijuana. Iggy's twin sat on the sofa, his head back. Except for a different colored T-shirt, Braden would have had a hard time telling them apart.

"Where were the two of you on Saturday evening?" she asked without wasting any time.

"Saturday," Iggy muttered. "Here probably."

"Yeah, here," Oden said.

"That's interesting because Millard Ingram said you two were with him at an after-hours party in the rodeo arena," Tessa said as she peered around the space, a look of disgust on her face.

"Yeah, we was there." Iggy dropped onto the sofa next to his brother. "Even have pictures of the night."

"Shut up, man," Oden said. "They could get you for breaking and entering."

"We're not interested in arresting you," Braden said. "Just in confirming Junior's alibi."

"You swear?" Iggy tried to focus but was unable to manage it.

Tessa nodded, and Iggy tapped his phone screen, then held it out with a picture holding Saturday's date stamp.

Oden swatted at the phone. "Don't be so stupid. Cops don't tell the truth. Junior's told us like a zillion times this one never does, so put that phone away."

"He does blame you for his prison time," Iggy said to her as he shoved his phone back into his pocket.

"I was just doing my job."

"Not according to Junior." Oden took over for his brother. "He thinks a more experienced deputy woulda figured out he didn't do nothing and let it go. But you're this do-good crusader, so you hauled him in."

"He hit his grandmother." Tessa's tone was hard and pointed. "You know it, and I know it. I can't believe you'd hang out with a guy like that."

"That's your version of the story," Oden snapped.

Tessa widened her stance. "Okay, fine. You may think he didn't hit his grandmother, but you have to know he's capable of stealing a bull and letting it loose in an arena, right?"

"Priceless." Iggy started laughing, soon unable to breathe until he got it under control and looked at Oden. "'Member when that ranch foreman was riding Junior's back, and he sicced that bull on him?"

Oden joined his brother in laughter.

"Wish I'da been there." Iggy slapped his knee. "Junior said he'd never seen the guy run so fast. Had to climb the corral fence to get away."

So Junior had done something like this before. And he clearly wished Tessa ill. They'd gotten the very answers they'd come for, and Braden didn't want to spend another second in that rat hole of an apartment. He strode to the door and opened it for Tessa.

Once she pulled the door closed, he turned to her. "The picture confirms Junior's reason for his prints, but I feel like there's more going on here."

She nodded. "He could have partied at the arena on purpose so he'd have a reason for why his prints showed up on the lock."

Braden opened the truck door. "And it's clear

he tried to harm someone with a bull before, so it wouldn't be far-fetched to think he'd do it again."

"Exactly." She slid into the passenger seat.

"How about we grab some lunch and review each suspect before deciding how to proceed?"

"Lunch sounds good, but with everything that's been going on, people are likely to ask a ton of questions at a restaurant. Mind if we head back to the ranch to eat?"

"Are you kidding? Your nana's cooking? I'm all over that." He grinned at her.

Instead of looking away or ignoring him as she'd done on the drive over, she returned his smile with a broad one that lit up her eyes, and his heart somersaulted. He liked the feeling. The warmth. Liked it far too much for his own good.

Her phone rang, breaking the connection, and she lifted it to her ear. "What do you have for me, Randy?"

Braden tried to hear what the fingerprint examiner had to say, but her volume was too low.

"Okay. Any other prints return a match yet?" Her face screwed up in concentration, then she frowned. "Keep me updated."

She stowed her phone. "Cliff Falby's prints from my phone don't match any of the prints I lifted from the arena."

"Doesn't rule him out, though," Braden said.

"He could still be involved in stealing the bull, but either wore gloves or wasn't the man who actually cut the lock."

FOURTEEN

The night was overcast and hazy, but the arena barn glowed with overhead lights as Tessa pulled Copper's cinch tight and patted his neck.

"Two more runs," she whispered. "And if we're to go out as winners, we have to make them both count. Ready to do this, fella?" She leaned closer to her beloved friend. "I know you love barrel racing. Me, too. But after this rodeo, it's not in the cards for us anymore. I still love you. Always will."

He rubbed against her hand, bringing tears to Tessa's eyes. She had to work hard to keep her emotions under control. She glanced up to see Braden eyeing them from the doorway where he'd been standing watch. After last night's incident, he'd been even more tense and guarded, but right now his tender expression said he understood her angst.

A soft smile lightened his look, and the honest sincerity of his response instantly caught her up.

This wasn't one of his shallow flirtatious smiles. It was deep, filled with meaning, and it made her want to step closer. Maybe kiss him again—but that was dangerous thinking that could only result in a broken heart.

Her phone rang, snapping his gaze free. She was thankful and irritated at the same time.

"Matt," she answered when she saw his name on the screen. "What's up?"

"I just received an anonymous text about a man in the arena who could be behind the attacks. I have the guy in sight and need you to come up here to see if you recognize him."

"Now?" She glanced at the horseshoe-shaped clock on the wall. "It's almost time for my run."

"Then you better make it quick."

She wanted to tell him to forget it, as she didn't want to risk being late, but this could be the break they'd been hoping for. "I'm on my way."

"What is it?" Braden's voice held a worried edge.

She explained. "We have just enough time if we hurry."

"I don't know." He frowned. "This could be a trap."

"We don't have any solid leads and we can't afford not to check it out."

He searched her gaze for what seemed like

precious minutes. "We'll have to leave Copper here—we can hardly take him into the stands."

She quickly ran through the schedule. If she was late, she would incur a time penalty that she could never overcome to win the championship. Finding her attacker was more important, though. She had to check this guy out.

She closed the stall door. "I'll be back in a flash, Copper."

"Not such a flash that you don't keep an eye out for the attacker," Braden warned.

"I'll be careful."

"And you'll be at my side." He put his arm around her waist and drew her tight against his hip.

She loved the solid feel of his body next to her and had only one problem with his hold. "It's gonna be hard to move quickly like this."

"Tough. It's the way it's going to be." With his unyielding tone, she'd spend more time arguing with him than the time they'd lose by the awkward gait.

She set off, and he had no choice but to come along or lose contact. Tessa smiled at the volunteer standing watch at the gate for the barn area. Across the street, she wove in and out of the crowd, making good time despite being joined at the hip with Braden. Inside, the announcer's voice caught Tessa's attention for a moment, and her footsteps faltered when she heard him talk about the standings.

"If you want to make your run on time, we need to keep moving," Braden said.

She searched the stands and spotted Matt waving about halfway up the bleachers. Due to the crowd, Braden had to move behind her as she climbed the steps. He hooked a finger though one of her belt loops, as if he felt a need to be connected to her.

As they moved, spectators called out Braden's name. He shouted back his greetings, but she doubted he lost focus on protecting her. That was just the kind of man he was proving to be. Dependable. A man she could count on. A man she'd gained tremendous respect for. A man she was falling for more and more as time passed, and she didn't know what to do about it.

Her phone rang and seeing Kendall's icon, Tessa stopped and answered.

"I know you're getting ready for your run," Kendall said, "but I thought you'd like to know I talked to Jason. He's doing Cowboy Christmas like you thought. Riding with a couple of other guys who confirmed his alibi for both days."

"Thanks for checking," Tessa said, drawing Braden's interest. "I really appreciate it."

"He asked about you. Made it sound like he wanted to get back together."

Just the thought made her angry. "I hope you told him that was never happening."

"Oh, I told him that and a few other things while I had a chance." Kendall laughed and disconnected.

Tessa faced Braden. "Kendall confirmed Jason is out of town."

"And what did you mean when you said that was never happening?"

"He hinted at getting back together. No way that's going to happen." Normally, she'd follow that declaration by saying she wasn't going to start dating anyone else, either…but for some reason, the words wouldn't come. Not something she was going to think about now.

She hurried up to Matt. "Which guy is it?"

Matt stared straight ahead. "Three rows up from us. Section C. Sitting to the right of the guy wearing the black hat with a red-and-white band."

Tessa located the suspect and took in his features. "I've never seen him before, but his build and height are right for my attacker at the barn."

Matt gave a quick nod. "He's not the least bit nervous with us standing here. So if he *is* our guy, he's one cool customer."

"We're far enough away that he might not think we even notice him."

"Either way, I'm going to ask him some questions."

"I'd like to stay and help, but I need to go before I incur a penalty."

"Go get 'em, sis." He squeezed her shoulder. "Check in with me afterward, and I'll let you know what I discover."

She nodded but wasted no time easing her way down the bleachers and back outside the arena, where Braden pulled her close to his side again, and they both kept their gazes roving. Thankfully, they arrived back at the barn with no problems.

Copper whinnied at the sight of her. "Hey, I didn't forget about you. But we have to hurry now."

She led him out of the stall.

"Keep alert," Braden warned as he came alongside them. "Don't let leading Copper distract you."

She nodded and the three of them took the same path back toward the arena. She was worried about the time and wanted to rush ahead, but she had to calm herself. Not only to stay safe but also so she didn't make Copper jittery.

At the contestant entrance, she mounted, and

Braden patted her leg. "Make this the run of your life."

She nodded and trotted inside to get in line behind Felicia, who was just approaching the alleyway. Tessa couldn't have cut it much closer. Maybe that was the whole purpose of the call. Felicia could have sent the text to keep Tessa from arriving on time. Seemed underhanded, but Tessa just didn't trust the woman.

Felicia took off and turned in a decent time, leaving her in second place, but Tessa wasn't worried. It was a time she and Copper could easily beat. She bent over his head. "We've got this, fella. We can beat Felicia in our sleep."

She eased him forward and then pulled in a deep breath and took off, racing for the first barrel. Copper's feet pummeled the soft soil. The wind sailed through her hair as adrenaline sent her heartbeat skyrocketing. She was alive and flying.

She reached the first barrel. Leaned in. Started around. Reached the far side. A loud snap sounded. Her saddle slid to the side and released from Copper's back. She plummeted toward the ground. Tripped up Copper. He went down.

"No!" she screamed as her head slammed into the barrel and the ground came up to meet her.

Tessa's scream tore at Braden's heart as he made his way to the alleyway gate, where the volunteer in charge of security gave him a warning look to stay back. Forced to stay in place, he kept his eyes locked on Tessa, mentally willing her to be all right.

"Get up," Braden whispered. "Please be okay and get up."

She didn't move. Not an inch.

Copper got back on his feet. Circled around and bolted for the next barrel. He was finishing the race without her.

"Please, Tessa," Braden begged. "Get up."

No movement. She was hurt. She needed him. Not even one beat passed before he was on the move. Sure, medical personnel were already crossing the arena to get to her, but he didn't care. He *had* to be there with her.

He vaulted the rail. The burly volunteer grabbed his arm.

Braden broke free and barreled down the alleyway. A rodeo employee had snagged Copper's reins and stood near the exit, his expression somber. Braden charged across the sandy soil. The doctor was kneeling by Tessa, examining her, and Braden couldn't see her face. His gut cramped hard.

Her foot moved. Just a fraction. Then the other. She was alive!

Thank You, Father.

He reached her. Her eyes were open and the

doctor was running his hands over her body, checking for injuries.

"Copper, where's Copper?" she called out. "Is he okay?"

"A volunteer has him and he looks fine." Braden dropped to the ground to take her hand. "I'm here, darlin'. Are you okay?"

A weak smile tipped the corners of her mouth. "I'm fine. Just got the wind knocked out of me."

"Looks like you may be right," the doctor said. "But you hit the barrel with your head, so I'd like to do a complete neurological exam to rule out a concussion. Can you walk to the medical tent or do we need a stretcher?"

"I can walk." She started to get up.

Braden was having none of it. He scooped her into his arms and started for the sidelines. She tried to squirm free, but he held fast.

"Relax," he said. "Enjoy the ride."

"There you have it, folks," the announcer's voice boomed over the speakers. "That's former PBR champion Braden Hayes performing a hero's rescue."

The crowd went wild. Coming to their feet, applauding and shouting their approval at Braden. Tessa relaxed, and he hoped she'd changed her mind about his help.

Walt bolted from the stands and jogged across the field. "How's my Peanut?"

"I'm fine, Dad. Just got the wind knocked out of me."

"Then why can't you walk?"

"I can, but…" She looked up at Braden.

Her father met Braden's gaze and a sudden dawning of understanding appeared in his eyes. "I see how it is. That okay with you, Peanut?"

"The crowd loves it, so I don't want to disappoint them."

"Then I'll take care of collecting Copper and your saddle." He gave Braden a tight look that said, "Don't hurt my daughter," and the intensity in Walt's gaze tightened Braden's gut.

"I want a report on how Copper's doing the minute you know anything," she called after her father.

"You got it." He turned to the arena and gave a thumbs-up. He was most likely signaling the rest of Tessa's family, but the crowd took hold of it and their cheers grew.

"Your dad must have been good at scaring off guys who wanted to date you," Braden said as he continued across the arena.

Her eyebrow arched.

"You saw the look he just gave me."

"Yeah, but we're not dating. Nothing even close to it."

She was correct, and he had nothing to offer in response, so he kept his mouth shut. Besides, having a personal discussion while walking across an arena with hundreds of fans watching was a recipe for disaster.

He backed into the medical tent to split the flaps. She immediately squirmed free and dusted herself off as if brushing away his touch.

"Have a seat." The doctor gestured at a folding chair.

Tessa complied. Braden waited for her to ask him to leave and give her some privacy, but she didn't, so he perched on the edge of a table to wait. He'd been examined for concussions enough times to know the doctor would check her vision, hearing, reflexes and balance and ask her questions to show her memory wasn't impaired and prove that she could concentrate.

She probably knew the drill, too. People thought barrel racing wasn't a dangerous sport, but put a rider on a horse moving at top speed to circle barrels and falls weren't uncommon. But maybe this was more than an accident. Maybe their suspect tampered with her equipment. Wouldn't surprise Braden, but he hated to think it had happened under his watch. How he hated it. He'd check out her gear the minute the doc said she was okay.

She was fortunate if a concussion was her only injury. Sure, she'd have to sit out the rest of the competition, but Copper could have fallen on her. Stepped on her. And he could have gotten hurt, too.

The accident, maybe sabotage, replayed in Braden's mind. The cinch snapping and her saddle giving way. Her body plunging toward the ground. Slamming into the barrel. He'd hated it. Every second. He was glad this was her last competition. He had no right to be glad, though. Or care. Not when, despite the feelings he'd developed for her, he wasn't able to commit. That would just be cruel.

What if you could change? The thought came out of left field.

Or had it? He'd seen the strong McKade marriages proving a good marriage was possible with the right kind of commitment. The right people. And he loved their sense of family and being there for one another. Even admitted to himself that he would like to have a family and community like that. Could he change to have this in his life? Was it possible?

If so, they could get to know each other. Maybe start a relationship. Get married. He saw himself living here in Lost Creek with her. Maybe using his rodeo money to buy a ranch of their own. Working for her dad. Then coming home after a hard day to see her soft, sweet smile meant only for him.

The thought filled him so completely that he

sighed. He wanted it all. That was now clear. But what would happen in the long run? Would Tessa's smile remain so sweet or turn into a bitter smirk like the one his mother had developed? Like his father? Would their warm connection turn to bickering into the wee hours of the night until they finally split up only to repeat the process over and over again with different people?

His parents claimed they'd once been in love, but for as long as he could remember, bitterness over life's regrets had replaced what had presumably been the same kind of attraction he was feeling for Tessa.

He thought of the McKades again and their loving family. They were one of the few who had made it. It was a fluke, right? An exception. Especially for Braden. He'd never had love modeled for him, so what made him think he could have what the McKades had? He wasn't sure he was even capable of the kind of love a woman like Tessa deserved.

Tessa still felt the sting of embarrassment from the very public display of Braden's rescue. She wasn't used to drawing attention to herself other than during her run—where she was too busy riding to notice. But she also had to admit that she loved having a man caring enough to watch her back and carry her from the arena.

She glanced at him and saw the ongoing compassion and concern in his eyes. She liked his attention and liked having him around. She could no longer deny it, but how on earth was she going to deal with that revelation?

And what about the broken cinch? It was in good shape when she'd saddled Copper and shouldn't have snapped. So someone had to have cut it while they were in the stands. Meaning another attempt on her life.

"Well, young lady," the doctor said, "you're cleared to return to the competition. If you develop a headache, blurry vision or vomiting, head straight to the ER. We'll image your brain for any possible bleeds or swelling."

"Got it. Thanks, Doc." She came to her feet, and Braden rushed to her side as if he planned to help her walk.

"I'm fine," she said, more tersely than he deserved.

"Still, you should probably rest."

"Right. Like you rested every time you took a fall from a bull."

"Well, no, but—"

"I need to check on Copper. Make sure he's not injured."

"Your dad—"

"Doesn't know Copper the way I do."

"I'm not going to win this argument, am I?"

Instead of the frustration she'd expected, she saw a glint of humor in his eyes.

"Not a chance." She started for the exit and heard him catch up.

"Let's not be so eager to check on Copper that we forget to take precautions on the way to the barn. After all, I doubt the cinch failing was an accident."

She nodded. The announcer's voice rang through the night as the competition resumed. It suddenly dawned on her that the fall had taken her out of the running for the championship. So it was with a heavy heart that she headed for the back exit and down to the barn. Her dad had settled Copper in his stall, but her father wasn't in the barn.

She went straight to Copper. "I'm sorry, fella. I wanted us to win, but it wasn't God's plan for us."

She ran her fingers over his body, his legs, looking for any injury.

"Everything look okay?" Braden asked.

"So far, so good, but I want him checked out. Our vet's working the rodeo, so I'll give him a call." She dialed Hank, and he quickly agreed to examine Copper.

Tessa let out a sigh of relief, but when her father—face tight with anger and her saddle over his shoulder—stepped into the barn, her worry returned. Did he know something about Copper? Was he hurt and her dad had come to tell her?

Panic raced along her nerve endings.

"What is it?" she asked and braced herself for the answer.

He stepped over to her and held out her saddle. "It's official. Your fall wasn't an accident. Someone cut the cinch."

FIFTEEN

Braden watched Tessa pace in front of Copper's stall. Time seemed to tick by slowly as they waited for the vet. Braden thought to take her into his arms, but he suspected that would make her even more uneasy. Plus, Walt remained in the barn, and Braden would feel self-conscious comforting her with her father in the same space.

Voices sounded from outside, and he recognized the McKade women's chatter.

"Prepare yourself," Walt warned Tessa.

Betty, Winnie, Lexie and Kendall marched into the barn, all four of them going straight to Tessa. Gavin trailed behind them. Braden wondered where Jed and Matt were, but he assumed they had a reason for their absence. Tessa squirmed under her family's attention, but he loved seeing the way they circled her and hovered like worried hens until they were certain she was okay.

"The doctor cleared me," she said, easing back. "It's Copper I'm worried about."

"Is he hurt?" Winnie asked.

Tessa looked at Copper. "I don't know. Hank's on his way to check on him, but with you all hanging around fussing over me, it'll likely scare him off."

Winnie waved a hand at her daughter. "No need to exaggerate. We get the point. You want some space."

"Doesn't mean we're leaving, though," Betty added.

Tessa sighed. "I'll come home after Copper gets a clean bill of health and I'm able to trailer him."

"The sooner he's cleared, the better, but no need to take him home." Jed marched into the barn, a rifle over his shoulder and Echo at his heels.

"Granddad, what in the world?" Tessa gaped at him.

Braden felt his own mouth drop open and couldn't begin to guess Jed's plans.

"It's simple," he said, but Braden doubted carrying a rifle was that straightforward. "I'm going to spend the night right here in Copper's stall, and I brought Echo along for backup."

"But why?" Betty locked her gaze on Jed. "And for mercy's sake, why the gun?"

"Despite the volunteer manning the gate, someone got in here and sabotaged Tessa's saddle. So we play off that and set a trap. We leave Tessa's equipment and Copper here for the night, hoping to coax this bozo out of hiding, and I nab him."

"Granddad, I don't—" Tessa started to say, but a forlorn look replaced her grandfather's excitement.

"I appreciate your help," she said quickly, as if she knew he needed to be of assistance.

Braden applauded her grandfather's desire to offer his aid, and Tessa's kindness in obliging him, but it was unlikely that the suspect would return. He'd have to know they'd double-check every bit of equipment before her next run.

"So how did this creep get in here?" Gavin asked.

"There's no way to monitor every access point at night when you can't see the whole property," Walt said. "Not with the surrounding corrals and the exterior doors for every stall. And before we go blaming Harley for having only one guy on the gate, this is a small-town rodeo. There just aren't enough volunteers to keep an eye on every place that someone could gain access and there's never been a need."

"I don't blame him," Tessa said. "No one can totally secure an outdoor arena."

"He's taking this real hard," Walt said.

"As am I," Tessa said. "Copper could have been seriously hurt."

"Don't worry." Lexie circled her arm around

Tessa's back and hugged her. "Jed will keep an eye on everything and your next run will be safe."

If there was a next run. The thought left an ache in Braden's heart. On the one hand, he wanted her to give up on the competition for her safety. Especially since winning now was a long shot. But he'd gotten to know her. Knew the way she approached life with such tenacity, and he knew she'd do the run. He got that. Totally got it. He'd do the same thing and wanted to help her.

As the family worked out the specifics for Jed and Echo to stay, Braden stepped over to Kendall.

"Felicia turned in a pretty good time tonight," Braden said. "Any way you can see Tessa coming back from the fall to win?"

"Not unless Felicia isn't able to finish her run tomorrow night and that's unlikely."

"Do you suppose the committee would be open to hearing about the sabotage and letting Tessa run twice tomorrow?"

Kendall tilted her head in thought, looking like a spitting image of her mother. "Wouldn't hurt to try."

"While everyone waits for the vet to check Copper out, I'm going to head back to the arena to talk to Harley." Braden started to leave, then turned back. "Not a word of this to anyone. I wouldn't want them to get their hopes up only for it to fall through."

SIXTEEN

Tessa sighed out a breath of contentment and looked over the arena. Sunday morning had started as normal with the family gathered for breakfast before heading to church. This morning, however, they'd joined rodeo participants and their families for cowboy church. She loved the simple worship service held in the arena. Standing among the others, the sun shining from above, reminded Tessa of God's love, and nothing could dampen her spirits.

Okay, maybe Braden's reminder before they'd left the ranch to be cautious and aware today had darkened things a bit. Everyone agreed her attacker continued to show his preference to strike in the dark from places where he could easily evade capture, but that didn't mean they would let their guard down, even on a bright sun-drenched day.

She surveyed the arena from her perch off to the side. Matt stood at one entrance. Kendall at another and her father at the third. And Braden was at her side as usual. No one was getting to her here. Not this morning.

The Fourth of July parade later today might be another story, but she wasn't going to let the hint of unease ruin the last parade of her rodeo career. Her family would be working the event and would stage themselves along the route. In his PR role, Braden was already scheduled to ride Shadow and would be at her side.

She settled into her seat for the uplifting service. When it ended, she and Braden participated in an autograph signing on the field for several hours, then grabbed a quick lunch at the concession stand before making their way to the barn to saddle up Copper and Shadow.

Granddad slowly got up from a straw bale, stretching his back. "Seems like just yesterday that I could spend the night sittin' on a bale and not feel the effects. But now..." He shook his head. "Let's just say, I won't be riding a horse today."

Tessa hugged her grandfather. "Thank you for doing this."

"No worries." He smiled at her. "Just wish the bozo would've shown up so I could've given him what for."

"I know you do, Granddad. But now that we have the horses and equipment with us, you can go home and take a nap before you have to be back here to guard things again."

"Not on your life." He planted his hands on his still-trim waist. "I haven't missed a single parade with your nana since we got married and a little stiffness in the old joints isn't going to stop me today."

Tessa smiled at him. What an amazing man, husband, father and grandfather he was. He and Nana, her parents, too, were so committed to one another. Tessa loved that about them and knew now that someday she wanted to have that kind of relationship in her life.

She glanced at Braden, who was tightening Shadow's cinch. His brow was furrowed in concentration, his lips parted slightly as he breathed, reminding her of when he'd kissed her breathless and left her wanting so much more.

Did she want a long-term relationship with Braden? Something like her parents and grandparents shared? Was Braden the kind of guy she could connect with on that level?

He looked up and caught her watching him. A slow smile spread wide, and she responded with a smile of her own, never once thinking to stop. She'd grown comfortable with him. And boy, she had to admit that she wanted him to be around much longer than this weekend.

"You better git or you're gonna be late." Her

granddad's voice broke through her thoughts. "I'll take Echo with me."

Tessa snapped to attention and went to saddle Copper with her backup cinch. Once ready, she and Braden moved into position in the parade queue to wait for the event to begin. Copper danced, eager to get moving, but Shadow stood patiently.

"The parade is one of my favorite times of the year," she said to Braden. "I love seeing our community out in full force. Especially the excited kids. Does my heart good."

He studied her for a long moment. "Do you want to have your own children someday?"

She nodded. "But that would mean getting married and I don't know if I'm ready for such a commitment. What about you?"

"Me… Kids? No… I mean, just like you, I'd need to get married."

"And you're too busy playing the field for that to happen, right?" she said as a joke, but deep down she needed him to ease her mind over his past.

"What?" His brow furrowed.

"You like to flirt like Jason does," she said. "Before we got together, he always had girls hanging around him, too. He told me those girls weren't the marrying kind and I was. Turns out he wanted them and me both."

"Then he's a fool!" Anger flared in his eyes. "Sorry. I shouldn't have gotten mad, but he shouldn't have hurt you. He was right about one thing, though. Many of the women who hang around rodeos aren't the kind of women you'd take home to meet your mother. They're more like the ones my dad dated."

"Your dad?" she asked, totally fascinated now.

Braden sat watching her, and she suspected he was trying to decide if he could trust her with additional information about his past. He gave an almost imperceptible shrug and took a long breath. "After Dad split with Mom, he brought home different women all the time."

He shook his head as if the memory was distasteful. "Some stayed longer than others. He even married a few, but all of them lived to party and have a good time. Until Dad's money ran out, which it always did. Then they were out of there, looking for their next free ride."

He paused and clenched his jaw. "I hated having them around. Hated their cheap perfume. The way they pretended to be my mom. When I got older, I really hated some of them coming on to me instead. It was awful. I've always said to myself if I ever lost my mind and decided to get married, it wouldn't be to one of these women. It would be to someone good and caring. Warmhearted and strong, like you."

His compliment brought heat to her face, but her thoughts backed up a beat. "You said *if* you ever lost your mind and decided to get married. Guess that means you think marriage is crazy."

He gave a resolute nod. "My parents were the poster couple for everything wrong with marriage, and I don't aim to spend my life like them."

"But you—"

"Time to move," the parade organizer announced. "Let's get these horses going. And for crying out loud, Tessa and Braden, smile or you'll scare the kids."

Tessa got Copper going and plastered a smile on her face, but inside she felt like she was dying. Sure, she understood Braden better now and had come to recognize there was great depth to the man she once thought to be superficial.

Still, it didn't matter, did it? He claimed he wasn't the marrying type, so no matter her feelings, he'd told her there wouldn't be a relationship with him.

Not now. Not ever.

Something about the discussion with Tessa was niggling at Braden, and he wanted to ponder it, but his concern for her safety required all his concentration. He kept his head on a swivel as they progressed down the crowd-lined street, his hand shooting to his sidearm every time someone darted out of the crowd. He was so grateful that Texas had an open carry law, meaning he didn't have to conceal his gun, which would have slowed down his access. Thankfully, Tessa also carried, her gun snug in an ankle holster, but access to her weapon would take time, so he felt a greater responsibility toward her, and he wouldn't let her down.

Not even when parade-goers called out his name and waved. He smiled and waved back but never once let it distract him from the mission at hand. Each minute of the route felt like an hour, and after what seemed an eternity, they reached the end without a hitch.

Autograph seekers waylaid their departure and other parade participants passed them by, but they finally got going and turned down the road toward the barn. Predicted thunderstorms had held off, but ominous clouds ahead said the storm would arrive soon.

Tessa glanced at her watch. "I have enough time to take Echo for a quick walk and head over to the lab to clean the shoe print cast before my run."

"Looks like rain, so we best get a move on."

They wound as fast as they could in and out of spectators heading to the carnival rides, games and food stands that were set up in a nearby park. The first rodeo event of the day, a clown show, was scheduled in another hour, so when they reached the arena, the lot was all but deserted and they could make better time.

Several clowns hung around the parking lot and others on horses headed for the arena. Braden had a special fondness for these men who served as bullfighters to distract bulls and bucking broncs from injuring the riders.

Tessa dismounted at the barn, and when she entered the building, Braden relaxed for a moment. Jed had already returned and was sitting on the bale, petting Echo's head.

"Did you enjoy the parade?" Tessa asked her granddad as she led Copper into the stall.

"Sure enough did." He lifted his hat to scratch a thick head of gray hair.

Tessa started removing Copper's tack. "Thanks for agreeing to keep an eye on Copper this afternoon so I don't have to trailer him."

"Welcome." Her granddad's eyes burned bright.

Braden suspected it was pride from feeling useful.

"I hope I'm able to still serve others when I'm your age, Jed," Braden said and meant it. "You're a great role model."

His color darkened as if embarrassed, but he pulled his shoulders into a straight line.

Tessa removed Copper's saddle. "We're going

to take Echo for a quick walk before heading to the lab."

At the word *walk*, Echo's head popped up.

"You go on," Jed said. "I'll take care of the horses."

"Are you sure?" Braden asked. He felt as if he was taking advantage of this family enough as it was.

"It may come as a surprise, but I like grooming horses, so it'll be no hardship for me." Jed slapped his hat back on his head and patted Copper. "Looks like he could use a good cooling down. I'll take them both out to the corral to hose them down."

"Thanks again, Granddad." Tessa faced Echo and patted her leg. "Come, girl."

Echo jumped up, her shiny black tail wagging, and she zoomed to the barn door, pausing for a moment to look back at Tessa. She signaled with her hand, and Echo trotted back to Tessa's side. "That's a good girl."

The three of them set out, but they hadn't gotten far when Echo growled at a clown sitting on his horse. Braden had to smile at the guy's oversize jeans held up by suspenders over a red-and-white-striped shirt. He also wore a tattered straw hat with a bright red flower and had a large lasso hanging over his shoulder.

"Echo," Tessa chastised and gave the clown an apologetic look. "She's not fond of clowns."

He shrugged and smiled as if dogs often reacted negatively to him.

Tessa put her hand over her eyes to peer ahead. "Let's head out into the empty field, where Echo won't bother the other clowns in the parking lot."

They turned back and moved around the barn. Braden hated being in the same location where Tessa had been attacked the other night. The sun shone down bright today, but a cold chill slithered down his back.

They had gone only a short distance when Echo suddenly stopped moving and cocked her head. Braden scanned ahead, then to the side. Was about to turn back, when a lasso dropped over his chest and tightened.

What in the world? Was the clown playing a joke? Wouldn't be a surprise, but Braden couldn't risk it. He reached for his sidearm. The rope was jerked hard, preventing him from grabbing his gun. He was pulled off his feet, then dragged back.

Tessa's eyes went wide. Any other woman would have screamed, but she was a deputy, and law enforcement officers didn't lose their cool like that. She dropped to her knee, and he knew she was going for the gun in her boot.

Braden rolled to see that the clown from before had indeed tossed the rope. He'd secured it to the saddle horn and was holding a gun on Tessa.

"Don't move, Tessa," the clown said, the threatening voice belying the painted smile. "Nor would I call for help. And tell your dog to sit or I'll shoot your cowboy."

"Sit. Stay." Tessa held out her hand, and Echo complied.

The clown dismounted and tossed a shorter rope with a bandanna tied on the end to Tessa. "Put the bandanna in your friend's mouth. Then tie his hands up nice and tight."

She stood up but didn't move any farther, her eyes fearful. Then she shifted her gaze to Braden as if looking for advice.

The clown waved his gun. "Wait any longer and I shoot him."

Tessa suddenly moved into action and squatted next to him. She lifted her hand as if she planned to reach for his holster.

"Touch the gun and he dies," the clown said.

Braden smiled at her. "It's okay. Do as he says. I'll be fine." He lowered his voice. "Try to get away the minute you can."

"Shut up," the clown snapped.

"I'm so sorry for having to do this," she said, her eyes awash with tears.

"It'll be okay, darlin'." He smiled to ease her worry, but his gut was in a tight knot. If only he could figure out this guy's identity, but his wig, nose and makeup obscured any hope of figuring it out. Still, Braden didn't think his voice was that of Falby or Ingram.

She knotted the bandanna around his head, then tied his hands with the short rope.

"Now tie the lasso to the fence post," the clown demanded.

Tessa complied and the clown came closer to pull on the knots, making them even tighter. Braden glared up at the clown and wished he could yell at him. He grinned down at Braden and jerked his gun from his holster. He tucked it into a big pant pocket.

Echo got to her feet and started for Tessa. The clown spun. Waved his gun. "Get that dog under control again."

"Sit," Tessa said.

Echo obeyed and tilted her head to peer at Tessa. The sweet dog knew something was wrong, but she was so highly trained that she still obeyed Tessa's commands.

"Tie the dog to the fence," the clown demanded.

Tessa knelt beside Echo to pet her neck and give her head a kiss.

"Stop delaying." The clown put a boot in Tessa's back and shoved her forward.

Echo bared her teeth and growled. Rage colored Braden's vision red, and he tugged at his rope. If he could get free, he'd strangle the man with it.

"It's okay, girl," Tessa said. "You get to stay here with Braden, and I know you love being with him."

Her back to the clown, she tied Echo close by and gave Braden a pointed look, checking to see if he'd noticed that she'd put the knot on Echo's leash within his reach. He responded with the barest of nods and followed it by a look of apology. He'd let her down.

She squeezed his knee. "I'll be fine."

"Get up," the clown snapped as he backed up to his horse and mounted one-handed, his focus and gun not leaving Tessa's face. "I'm going to move to the fence. Use the rails to get on the horse in front of me. No funny business or I'll kill your doting detective."

Her lingering look for Braden tore at his heart. She climbed the railing and mounted in front of the clown. He continued to keep his gun aimed at Braden while she got settled. She probably could have disarmed the clown but not before he got off a shot. Braden knew Tessa would never put his life in danger.

The clown grabbed the reins and whipped the horse around. With a swift kick to the mare's flank, they galloped across the field, taking all hope of rescuing Tessa away in the blink of an eye.

SEVENTEEN

The moment the clown turned his back, Braden grabbed Echo's leash and freed the knot.

Run to Jed, girl. Go. Braden wished he could shout it to Echo, but the gag prevented him from speaking.

Echo took off running. Not toward Jed, but across the field after Tessa.

No. No. No. Now what?

God, please. Help me. Help us. Keep Tessa safe.

He struggled to free himself but couldn't budge the knot around his hands or the bandanna in his mouth. The clown had seen to that.

Braden heard a noise at the far end of the barn and turned to see Jed step out with Copper. He slammed his boots into the ground to make noise so Jed would hear his feet pound the packed soil and rustle though the grass. Still not looking, Jed bent to pick up the hose and Braden frantically stomped his boots some more. Finally, Jed looked in his direction, caught sight of him and came running. He dropped to the ground to undo the bandanna, all color in his deeply tanned face fading.

Braden told him about the clown. "He's got Tessa. Get my hands free, and I'll go after her in the truck."

"I'm coming with you." Jed worked on the knot at Braden's wrists.

"No. I need you to find Walt or Matt to mount a search-and-rescue team."

Jed was silent for a moment. "Don't much like staying here, but you have a point."

The moment Braden's hands were free, he jerked them around front and massaged his wrists. Jed started working on the lasso knot.

The rope loosened, and Braden shot to his feet. He bolted for Tessa's truck. His hand shook as he inserted the key, but he got the truck moving forward and across the empty field to the far parking lot. A thick crowd arriving for the clown show blocked his way, but he laid on the horn while frantically searching the crowd for her.

No sign of the horse, the clown, Tessa or Echo.

Braden lowered his window and leaned his head out. "Anyone see a woman and clown on a horse come through here?"

"Yeah," a guy yelled back. "Saw them turn onto Maple Street."

Braden remembered the street name from when they searched for the bull trailer, and he made his way there. In the distance, he heard sirens screaming and soon spotted Matt's patrol car at the next intersection. Braden shifted into Park and jumped out, jogging across the road to Matt.

"Anything?" he asked through Matt's open window.

Matt shook his head. "And it's killing me."

"Me, too," Braden said, his own frantic tone leaving him even more unsettled. "We have to hope Echo found Tessa and is helping. Or maybe her abductor hasn't found her gun and she can get to it."

Matt let out a low growl. "Why in the world did he change his MO and decide to abduct her in broad daylight? I mean, I'm glad he didn't shoot her on the spot, but that would've been easier than taking her."

"A gunshot would have brought everyone running, and he'd have been caught. Abducting her gives him a better chance of getting away with killing her. If only I could have made out the guy's identity. He didn't sound like Falby or Ingram."

"We can rule out Falby. Ernie called and said his daughter snagged her jacket in the trailer. She didn't tell anyone before because she wasn't sup-

posed to be playing anywhere near the trailers."
Matt's gaze drifted past Braden.

Braden turned to see Walt and Kendall rushing toward them. Braden spun and ran full tilt toward the pair, Matt right behind him.

"Do you have any idea where she is?" Braden clamped his hand on the back of his neck.

"We don't know," Kendall said. "But I was just about to tell Dad that I have an idea of who took her."

"Who?" Braden demanded.

The same worry threatening to stop Braden's heart filled her eyes. "I just finished the update for our fingerprint database, and it included a match for one of the prints from the lock. It belongs to Lemanuel Lankford. He's recently been arrested for a few drunk and disorderlies but wasn't in the system until I did the update."

Braden wanted to nudge her to speak faster. "You think this Lankford has Tessa?"

Kendall nodded. "He had a grudge against her."

"Explain," Braden demanded.

Walt cleared his throat, his gaze darting about as if he was unable to focus. "His wife was murdered about a year ago. Convenience store holdup—one of a string of similar robberies. In this last robbery, the clerk pressed a silent alarm and our deputy arrived on scene before the robber could take off. Unfortunately, he took Lankford's wife hostage and fled with her out the back door. Took her to a deserted running trail and strangled her."

"That's rough," Braden said and meant it, but he still could think only about Tessa. "And?"

"A surveillance camera captured the killer before he took off," Kendall said. "But he was wearing a ski mask, gloves, bulky clothes—there wasn't a lot there that we could use to identify him. We put the video on the evening news. Someone thought they recognized the medallion hanging from a chain around his neck, which led us to arrest Gino Crider."

Walt nodded. "But when we did a lineup, it all went south. We had them talk, and the store clerk said that Crider's voice sounded right, which was good for our case. Problem was, he's six foot three and all of the clerks said the robber was around five-six. And Crider had an alibi—though it was pretty flimsy. His girlfriend was willing to swear that he'd been with her at the time of the murder. We were about to let Crider go, but a jailhouse informant claimed Crider had confessed to him."

"But you still had the height discrepancy issue," Braden said, trying to move them along.

"Tessa offered to complete a photogrammetric examination of the video from the convenience store."

"What in the world is that?" Braden asked.

"Photogrammetry is the science of making determinations about objects in an environment based on visual evidence," Kendall said. "Tessa studied a still image from the surveillance footage and examined measurements of items in the store to estimate that the robber couldn't possibly be six feet tall, proving that Crider was innocent."

"By this time, Crider's preliminary hearing had started, and when we informed the DA of the test's results, the judge ordered Crider's release," Walt said. "Much to Lankford's dismay."

"Dismay?" Kendall repeated. "He was good and angry. Kill-someone angry."

"We worried he might take Crider out, but after all the bad press Crider got from the arrest and preliminary hearing, he decided to move way. So Lankford turned his anger on Tessa and declared the science behind her observation was bogus. Calling her out in public. Bad-mouthing her all over town. Phoning the office and demanding we let go of her theories and arrest Crider again. But he never made any actual threats against her."

"And now you think he has Tessa." Braden shoved a hand into his hair and felt like he was going to be sick. "Why didn't anyone think of him as the guy behind the attacks before?"

"Because we didn't think of a victim's family," Matt said. "Only criminals. Plus, it happened almost a year ago."

"And if you forget the drunk and disorderlies," Walt added, "which we believed was his response to losing his wife, he's a law-abiding citizen."

"*Was*, you mean," Braden said. "If he took Tessa, he clearly gave up on obeying the law."

He had her. The clown had her. A gun in her side, hidden under a big floppy clown sleeve—a warning not to call out or he'd shoot kids in the crowd, so she couldn't alert anyone to her predicament. She might risk her own life, but she'd never put a child in danger. He'd planned her abduction perfectly.

She could only hope that Braden would find a way to get free. She'd hated tying him up. Hated gagging him. She'd wanted to smooth his worried brow, give it a soft kiss and promise she'd be okay. But how could she promise such a thing when a crazed man held her at gunpoint?

They continued down side streets, trotting toward ominous clouds hanging in the distance. At the outskirts of town, he kicked the horse into a canter. She held the saddle horn to keep her balance, though she honestly considered falling off the horse and trying to flee. But then what? The creep would simply shoot her.

At least she still had her gun. She couldn't get to it while on the horse, but just knowing it was tucked in her boot gave her hope.

The clown jerked the horse reins to turn into a driveway. She caught a quick look at the name on the mailbox: *Lankford.* She knew that name. Knew it well.

"Mr. Lankford, is that you?" she asked.

He didn't answer, but the sudden stiffening of his body told her what she needed to know. The man who blamed her for his wife's killer going free had taken her captive. She'd done nothing wrong, but that never mattered to him. He'd still cursed her, his pain and anguish at losing his wife spewing out with his words.

How on earth was she going to reason with such a hurt and bitter man?

They rode up to a low ranch house secluded by towering trees. She had to believe he planned to kill her here.

"Get down," he demanded.

She took her time dismounting. He climbed off after her. A sudden gust of wind grabbed his hat, sending it swirling toward a large pickup in the driveway.

He made no attempt to retrieve the hat but tied the horse to the garage door handle.

"In the house." He shoved the gun into her back, pushing her forward.

Inside, the cooler temperature felt good, but nothing else about the place held any appeal. He'd let it go. Trash, dirty dishes. Soiled floors and furniture. A horrific odor permeating the air. She remembered how meticulous he'd once been about his grooming and perfectly pressed clothing. Maybe he'd quit caring. If he had, it didn't bode well for her.

He shed his red rubber nose and dropped his baggy pants to reveal a pair of blue jeans. Once free of the clown pants and shoes, he slid his feet into a pair of sloppily tied running shoes. She suspected they had a cracked sole, matching the print she'd found.

His gaze and gun remaining fixed on her, he moved across the room to grab a photo of his wife. He held it close to his chest and waved his gun at the door. "Out to the truck."

"Where are we going, Lemanuel?" She used his first name to make this personal and maybe get him talking.

"Shut up! You're not fit to use my name." He raised the gun as if planning to hit her, then suddenly changed his mind and used it to gesture again at the door. "Outside now."

She moved slowly, praying for help.

On the sidewalk, he pointed at the pickup. "In the truck."

She crossed the space, dragging her feet to stretch out the time.

He opened the passenger door. "Lie facedown on the seat so I can tie your hands."

She had to find a way to get him talking before he took her away. Maybe then she could learn something to help in freeing herself. "You've been trying to kill me for days. Why not just shoot me at the barn instead of this?"

He snorted. "And bring the cops running when they heard the gunshot? No way I'm going to jail for this. Not when it's something you deserve."

"I did nothing wrong."

"If you don't keep that trap shut, I'm going to gag you."

"But I really want the chance to explain photogrammetry again."

"Last warning. Shut up or I gag you."

"Okay, fine." She lay down on the dirty vinyl seat, panic having its way with her. She couldn't get to the gun in her boot, so she darted her gaze around, searching for any weapon she might get in her hands to use against him. Found nothing.

He jerked her arms behind her back and circled her wrists with rough rope. Before he could knot it, she kicked back at him hard and tried to sit up.

He groaned but remained in place, jerking the rope into a tight knot, biting into her skin. "Try that again and you'll wish you hadn't."

She continued to struggle, but he got the knot tied, then secured her legs and jerked her into a sitting position. With a shorter rope, he bound her upper body to the bucket seat and slammed the door. He got in and backed the vehicle around to leave. With a single-minded focus, he took them down the drive but stopped at the road to check for oncoming traffic.

Tessa frantically swung her gaze around for a way out. "Where are you taking me?"

"That's for me to know."

"You've gone through all this trouble to kill me. You must want me to know why you're doing this."

"All in good time." He pointed the truck toward town.

Town. Yes. Hope that someone would see them burgeoned, but they passed no one before he turned into a deserted park on the outskirts of Lost Creek. She recognized the area. How could she not when she'd been called out to a hiking trail here to work his wife's murder?

He parked at the trailhead, came around the truck to open her door and bent down to untie her ankles.

"You're going to kill me where your wife was murdered," Tessa said.

His head snapped up. Anger, raw and unfettered, in his glazed look made her suck in a breath.

"I was only doing my job," she said. "Crider didn't kill your wife, and he didn't deserve to go to jail."

"Says you and your mumbo-jumbo proof."

"It's not mumbo jumbo, but fact. Just like all the rest of the case. There was no solid proof against him."

"Shut up." He untied the rope from behind her chest and let it fall. "Out of the truck."

"Please," she said as she exited the vehicle, her hands still bound behind her back. "Let's talk about this."

"Nothing to talk about. My wife's dead, her killer is still walking around free and you're having a high old time in life while I can barely force myself to get out of bed."

"Maybe I can arrange to have the investigation reopened."

"Too late. Way too late." He shoved her forward just as big, fat drops of rain began to fall. "You're going to learn what it feels like to die a painful death as my wife did."

EIGHTEEN

Braden silently made his way toward Lankford's house from the south while Matt approached from the north. They saw the saddled horse tied to a handle on the garage, and next to it was a clown's straw hat, its ridiculous red flower beaten down by the rain, confirming they were in the right place.

Braden reached the corner of the house and glanced in the garage window. No vehicle. Had Lankford traded the horse for another mode of transportation? If so, they could be miles away by now.

The thought nearly made Braden lose it on the spot. He gulped in air and let it out. Cleared his fear and placed his back against the wall. He eased along the house to a picture window. He glanced inside. No movement, but he saw clown shoes and baggy pants lying on the floor. He skirted under the window and met Matt at the door.

"No vehicle in the garage," Braden whispered. "No sign of life in the family room, but I did see his clown pants and shoes."

"Let's look around back." Matt led the way.

Heart racing over what they might find, Braden followed. Weeds strangled the backyard, and bags piled high by the house emitted a rotting odor that took Braden aback.

Matt turned the knob on the back door. He cast a questioning look at Braden. "Exigent circumstances legally allow me access."

"Exigent or not, on duty or not, I'm going in with you and don't try to stop me." Braden brushed past Matt and entered a kitchen with dishes piled high in the sink. His shoes stuck to the filthy floor, giving off sucking sounds, but he soon reached a hallway with dirty carpet and his movements were deadly silent.

He caught a strong whiff of a cat's litter box. Seemed like this guy had given up on life. Let things pile up and stopped caring and cleaning.

Braden glanced into an empty family room, then signaled his intent to keep moving down the hallway. He shot a look into a bathroom, where he found the offending litter box but still no sign of a cat. He opened a hall closet. Cleared three bedrooms. All were empty except for boxes and trash that filled the space. The last room was larger, and Lankford had tacked pictures on the aged wood paneling, nearly filling an entire wall.

Braden approached and found snapshots of Tessa in various scenarios.

Matt joined him. "He's been following her. I recognize some of these and they're nearly a year old."

"Look at this." Braden pointed at her picture from last week's TV news story. Lankford had scribbled notes on the border about hating her for being alive and having fun at the rodeo when his wife was dead. "This could explain why he's taking action after all this time."

"Right, like he wanted to hurt her but never had the courage. Then he saw her on the news, happy and carefree, talking about unimportant things like a rodeo, while his wife had died. He came to the end of his rope and snapped." Matt's voice was low and filled with emotion.

Braden couldn't look away from the picture. From Tessa's wide smile. Her shining eyes. Her obvious love for barrel racing. And he even understood what had caused Lankford to snap. Love for his wife. Braden didn't agree with the man's actions, not at all, but Braden understood the love and grief he felt. Finally understood the love.

He'd never experienced how the depths of love could consume a man. But now he did. Thanks to Tessa. He wanted her safe. Desperately. The feeling overwhelmed him. He was a professional law enforcement officer, but his need for her to be safe had nothing to do with his profession. It had to do with his feelings for her as a woman. He liked her spunkiness and grit. Her heart for others. Her kindness. Actually, he loved pretty much everything about her.

He had to admit he was in love with her. And what had he done about it? Let his past fears keep him from thinking about a relationship with her. From telling her how he felt. All that, and he'd never once asked God to help him work through his issues.

What kind of a Christian did that make him?

Thunder rolled through the sky and driving rain beat against Tessa's body as she started up the steep incline. The water ran down the hard-packed trail and slippery mud took her down. Her hands tied, she couldn't break her fall and hit hard.

"Up." Lankford jerked the gun.

"You have to untie me if you want me to make it up this incline," she shouted at him in frustration.

"Not happening," he said, his gaze getting angrier. "I'll just shoot you right here if I have to."

He didn't want to kill her here, but Tessa truly believed if she gave him no choice, he'd pull the trigger. She maneuvered around until she could get to her feet and lowered her head to trudge forward.

Could Braden have figured out where she was? Be coming for her?

Braden, her hero. He'd been there for her all along. At each step, he'd stuck to her side, taking her safely through dangerous situations. She'd forever be grateful to him. But that wasn't all. Being alone like this—the alone she'd once thought was safest—told her she wanted him in her life. She loved him. Simple as that. But could she trust him?

Be strong and courageous. God's word in Joshua came to mind. He promised always to be with her, but He didn't say she wouldn't feel pain. Wouldn't suffer. After Jason, was she brave enough to risk telling Braden how she felt if she survived Lankford's rage? She hoped so.

A bolt of lightning flashed, and she saw something moving in the woods. She strained her eyes and spotted Echo easing through the scrub.

Tessa's heart soared but immediately fell. She loved seeing her faithful companion, but she didn't want Echo to get hurt. Tessa had to act fast to prevent it. She turned her back to the woods. Held out her hands to signal Echo to stay. She couldn't risk looking behind her to see if it had worked.

"Get moving," Lankford demanded.

She searched his gaze for any hint that he'd noticed Echo. His gaze was on the trail ahead and he clutched his wife's photo tighter.

Hoping to connect with him, Tessa tried to empathize with his emotions. "Being here must be hard on you."

He grunted.

"I'm so sorry for your loss," she said, making sure her sincerity flowed through her words.

His eyes fired daggers of anger at her, his running clown makeup making him even more scary-looking. "No, you're not. If you were, you would have convicted Crider, not taken his side. He killed Andrea. I know he did."

"Crider wasn't the killer. We weren't able to find the real killer. Sometimes, no matter how much we care, we can't catch the bad guy."

"Shut up and get moving." He pushed her ahead.

She glanced to the side. Saw Echo sitting as commanded. Good. She started forward, taking it slow, but they soon rounded a bend to the site she dreaded seeing again. Someone had pounded a memorial cross with drenched silk flowers into the ground where Andrea Lankford had died.

Tessa bit back her fear at reaching the place where he planned to kill her and asked, "Did you make this lovely memorial?"

He grunted again and pushed her over to a

large tree, where he shoved her down to the soggy ground. She scooted around until she could rest her back against the tree and look up at him. Thankfully, the tree canopy served as an umbrella and she could easily see his movements.

He stepped up to the memorial and gently placed his wife's picture near the flowers. He kept glancing at Tessa, but she used the time to look for a way to escape. She would have gone for her gun, but she couldn't get to it with her hands tied behind her. In the woods, she caught sight of Echo inching closer. Most dogs would full-out run into the space, but Echo's training taught her to listen and obey. Tessa had told her to stay back on the trail, and she likely thought she was being naughty now by having followed, so her movements were hesitant. The sweet dog took a few more steps before sitting, her tail wagging through the brush.

Tessa glanced at Lankford. He was staring at the picture, his shoulders heaving with sobs. He'd lost focus. She shifted to her side so she could signal to Echo again.

"What are you doing?" Lankford's accusatory voice snapped her head back to look at him.

"Nothing."

"Liar." He peered into the woods. "It's that dog of yours again. I can't have her causing a problem. Call her to you."

"No." Tessa raised her chin and prayed he didn't shoot her right on the spot.

"I'm a dog lover, and it would hurt real bad if I had to kill this one, but…"

"You don't have to do anything. This can all end now."

"I said call her." He lifted a foot and slammed it into her side.

Tessa tried not to cry out, but she couldn't contain the anguish and groaned.

Echo charged toward them. Reaching the clearing and launching herself into the air, she made contact with Lankford's body. Growled and chomped down on his wrist.

"Call her off!" Lankford lifted his arms to battle Echo.

With her hands tied, Tessa couldn't go for Lankford's gun or try to grab her own. Her best chance was to run. She struggled to her feet and bolted into the woods.

"Come, Echo," she called over her shoulder.

She heard Echo bounding into the woods. Lankford made good on his promise and fired, the boom reverberating through the trees and breaking Tessa's heart.

Natalie came into the conference room where Braden was meeting with Walt, Matt and Kendall to figure out how to locate Tessa. Natalie was carrying the shoe print Tessa had cast at the crime scene.

"I cleaned the cast," she said, worry obvious in her tone. "It's from a high-end Nike running shoe. The sole has a wide crack, so if we get close to Lankford, we might be able to track him in the mud."

"Running shoe," Braden said, something he'd recently heard swirling in the back of his mind, but he couldn't seem to lay hold of it.

He got up to pace and think.

C'mon. C'mon. C'mon. Think. Tessa's life could depend on it.

He tried harder. Ignored the others as they talked to Natalie. Thought. Zoned in. Suddenly, the memory became clear.

Running.

He spun to face the group. "What if Lankford took Tessa to the same running trail where his wife was murdered?"

"You mean like re-creating her murder?" Walt asked.

"Exactly."

Walt gave a clipped nod. "You may have something here."

"Something worth checking out. I'll head out there now."

"Not so fast." Walt flipped up a hand. "I know you want her found. So do I. More than you know.

But we can't go running off half-cocked. You'll need backup and a map of the park."

"I can print the map right now." Natalie stepped to a computer workstation in the corner.

"What if you're wrong?" Walt's voice broke.

Braden stared at him. This was the first time since Tessa went missing that Braden considered what Walt must be going through. Braden knew his own pain. Knew it with such intensity that he struggled to breathe. But Walt was her father. His suffering would be beyond measure.

Walt drew in a long breath through his nose and let it out through his mouth. "As much as I want to nail this guy, Matt will be a lot faster climbing that steep trail and can go with you. I'll stay here in case other leads come in."

"Roger that." Matt jumped up to grab the map from the printer. He laid it on the table and pointed at a location halfway up a small mountain. "There are two hiking trails here. The one where Andrea died and this other one." He ran his finger along another path. "They merge higher up."

"Odds are he took Tessa via the direct route," Braden said. "But he may have been trying to hide his tracks and taken the other one."

"Then we split up when we get there," Matt said.

"I have to insist that no additional deputies

are dispatched to the trail. Tessa's life is at stake, and we can't risk one of them giving Lankford any inkling that we're onto him. We have to be in stealth mode."

Matt nodded. "I'll grab radios, and we'll be on our way."

Braden felt the clock ticking down, and it seemed like an eternity before they were on the road, heading for the park, the wipers swishing through a steady rain. How must Tessa be feeling right now? Drenched to the skin. Alone with Lankford. Afraid. Thinking no one would come to her rescue. Maybe feeling hopeless.

Hopefully, she still had her gun. Maybe Echo had found her, too, giving her some hope.

God, please. I have to think You put us together for a reason. Keep her safe and let me get to her in time.

Braden saw the sign for the park ahead and they soon pulled into the parking lot to see a large truck parked at the trailhead.

Braden squinted through the rain, hoping to make out the plate number that they'd located when they'd run a background check on Lankford. "That's Lankford's license plate."

Matt shifted into Park. "I'll call Dad to let him know to send additional units to block off the park."

"Make sure they know to stay on the perimeter." Braden was out of the car in a flash, praying with each step up the path that he'd rescue Tessa long before any additional units arrived at the park.

The shot went wide, and Echo bounded up beside Tessa.

Thank You, God.

Together, they charged through the forest. Tessa feared a bullet in the back with each step, but she had no choice but to go on. She couldn't press lower branches aside. Not with her hands tied. They slapped at her body, stinging and bringing tears to her eyes.

She heard Lankford's footsteps much farther behind. She had a good head start and had to hope she would succeed in getting away.

The forest grew denser, and she had no choice but to slow down and ease in and out of trees. She reached a clearing and heard rushing water ahead. *Yes!* The river that flowed through town. If she could cross it, she might be able to get away.

She picked up speed and raced ahead. The land suddenly dropped off. Without her hands to balance, there was no way she'd get down the incline on her feet. She dropped to the ground and scooted down the hill. She skirted large rocks and shrubs. When the ground cleared, she lay on her side and rolled the remaining distance to speed up her movements. Echo came bounding over. The Lab nearly pounced on Tessa and gave her big sloppy kisses.

"No time for play," Tessa said. "We have to keep going and cross the river."

She got up and stepped into the rushing water. The strong current caught her feet, nearly unsettling her. She wobbled and finally gained her footing. Getting into running water without the use of her arms might not be the smartest move, but it was her only option.

She stepped in deeper. The current pressed at her knees. Her thighs. Waist. Echo paddled alongside her, giving Tessa some comfort. Thunder rolled through the skies and rain pummeled her head. The water churned in angry froths, and she was now seriously worried she wouldn't make it to the other side.

She risked a look back. Saw Lankford on the hill. His gun raised.

Father, please. Don't let me drown. Don't let Lankford hurt us. Please!

NINETEEN

Hidden in the forest, Braden poked his head around a tree to see a memorial made of flowers, a picture and a cross, but no sign of Tessa or Lankford.

Braden pressed his mic. "They're not at the target location. I heard movement in the woods south of here on my way up but figured Lankford wouldn't venture off the trail. I'll head south and check it out now."

"I'll intersect the trail in a minute or two." Matt's hard breathing came over the earbud. "There's an overlook there and I should be able to get a good view of the area."

"Report the minute you do."

Braden retraced his steps south. Rain started coming down in sheets now, making it hard to see very far ahead. Braden carefully picked his way down the slippery hill.

"I'm in location," Matt's voice came through Braden's earbud.

"And?" Braden whispered.

"Tessa broke free from Lankford. She's in the river heading east. Her arms are tied behind her."

"And Lankford?" Braden asked and held his breath.

"I don't see him."

A gunshot rang though the air.

The shot didn't come from Matt's rifle but a handgun.

Tessa.

Braden's heart refused to beat. She needed him. Needed him badly, and he wasn't there for her.

"Find Lankford," Braden said into the mic, then barreled through the woods until he reached a clearing. Lankford stood at the edge of an outcropping, his weapon still raised. Braden followed Lankford's line of sight. Saw the current carrying Tessa away.

No! He had to get to her. Now!

If he tried to tackle Lankford from behind to stop him, they'd both go tumbling over the edge. Didn't matter. It would stop Lankford from getting off another round and save Tessa if Lankford hadn't already shot her.

Braden bolted forward. Lankford heard him. Started to turn. Braden launched himself at him and grabbed Lankford around the neck. They fell off the craggy outcropping, the gun going flying. They hit hard. Lankford was ripped from

Braden's hands, but he didn't care as there was no way the guy could easily get back to his gun.

Braden's shoulder hit a rock. He raised his hands to protect his head and rolled down the rocky landscape, each hit bringing bone-jarring pain. So what? He might be sustaining multiple injuries, but he was getting to Tessa faster and could help her.

If he lived.

Tessa popped up. Dragged in a breath, but got more water than air. The current pulled her back under, and the cold water felt like a grave.

Is this it, Father? Am I going to die?

Panic seared her mind. She couldn't think. Couldn't act. Something came around her neck. Lankford? She bucked and tried to free herself. Her body was jerked up. Her head surfacing above the water. She gulped in air. Choked. Coughed. Tried for more air. Coughed again, her lungs burning.

"I have you, Tessa," Braden's deep voice penetrated her foggy brain.

Braden? He'd found her.

Oh, God, thank You!

She concentrated on gaining a full breath while the current continued to take them, but she felt safe in Braden's care and relaxed to go with the flow and lessen the drag on his arms.

"There's a downed tree ahead," Braden said, his voice strained with exertion. "I'll try to grab on."

"Lankford," she said, glad she could finally speak. "He has a gun."

"Matt's got him covered."

She felt Braden's body hit the tree hard and waited for them to go under. They didn't, but their movement downstream stopped. She squirmed around until she could see Braden's other arm around the tree.

"Face me so I can hoist you onto the tree." He loosened his hold enough for her to turn.

She kicked hard to rotate and caught sight of his face. His dear sweet face, his feelings for her burning in his eyes.

His gaze lingered. "I love you, Tessa. Love you with all my heart."

"I love you, too." She'd barely gotten the words out when his lips descended on hers. They were cold and warm at the same time, and she couldn't move. Didn't want to move, just wanted to revel in loving him.

Something poked her head from above. She pulled back and opened her eyes to look up. Echo sat on the tree, her snout pushed out. Her tongue came out to lick Tessa.

TWENTY

The next morning, Tessa sat astride Copper. Due to rain, the committee had postponed the rodeo, allowing her to make her last run. Sure, she wasn't going to win, but that was okay. She owed this final run to Copper and she wouldn't deny him the opportunity to show what he could do—she would give her very best effort, for him. Her whole body ached from all that she'd gone through, but she'd ridden with more painful injuries in the past, and she could do this today.

She bent low over Copper's head. "Let's make this a run to remember."

She pointed him into the arena and had to admit she missed having Braden at her side. She didn't miss the danger that had put him there, but she missed his company. They'd declared their love again last night before she'd had to go to bed or fall asleep in her chair. She wished they could have had more time alone to talk about their future, but honestly, having the extra time apart would help her gather her thoughts over their sudden declarations.

She heard the announcer call her name for the pre-run introduction of the final six contestants, and she moved into the arena and took her spot behind the other riders. Even with the fall, she was in fifth place.

"Ladies and gentlemen, we have a special announcement before we begin the barrel racing competition and here to tell us all about it is former PBR champion Braden Hayes."

Tessa's gaze flew to the announcer's booth and spotted Braden. He was supposed to be sitting with her family. What in the world was he doing up there?

"It's my pleasure to tell you," his deep voice boomed over the speakers, "that I petitioned the rodeo officials on behalf of Tessa McKade after her spill Saturday night."

She gasped, drawing the attention of her fellow riders, who were all smiling, except Felicia.

"You may have heard that a man was trying to kill Tessa," Braden continued. "And he cut through her cinch to cause her to fall. What you don't know, and I hope Tessa doesn't hate me for mentioning, is this is her last competition."

The crowd seemed to gasp in unison, but not the other barrel racers. Obviously, they'd somehow known before his announcement, but how, she had no idea. She hadn't told anyone but Braden and her family. She didn't like all this attention and hadn't planned to announce her retirement in a large crowd like this, but she didn't mind Braden mentioning it if he had a good reason.

"You see," he said, a hush falling over the arena, "her horse has medical issues and can't continue, so though she doesn't want to quit, she's going to. We all understand that, right? Her wanting to protect Copper."

The crowd applauded and heat rushed up Tessa's neck.

"Anyway," Braden went on, "the fall on her last run wasn't due to any mistake on her part, and so I asked the officials to offer her an extra run tonight to make up for it. At first, they said it wouldn't be fair to the other barrel racers who've had things out of their control happen in the past, too. But then the committee asked the other racers for permission for Tessa to run again and each of them agreed."

Tessa's mouth fell open, and she shot a look at Felicia, who for once didn't send daggers in Tessa's direction. She didn't seem pleased—but she didn't seem angry, either. She was likely happy to hear Tessa was retiring and could have felt pressured by the others to agree to Braden's request.

"So we'll be starting tonight's competition with a makeup run by Tessa McKade."

The crowd came to their feet, cheering and clapping.

Tessa stood in her stirrups and took a bow, then looked up at Braden and smiled. It hit her then. Right between the eyes. He wasn't the kind of man who would cheat on a woman he loved. He was the kind of guy who would go the extra mile. Do the unexpected. Cherish the woman he loved. The only question in Tessa's mind now was did he love her enough to let go of his relationship phobia?

"So without further ado," the announcer's voice came over the speaker and snapped Tessa free of the lock Braden's gaze had on her. "Let's clear the field so Tessa can take her first run."

Tessa trotted Copper out of the arena. Her heart was overflowing with gratitude, and she called out her thanks to the other racers for this chance as she moved into place in the alleyway. After a few deep breaths, she kicked Copper's flanks and he took off flying. He started faster than he ever had before, and she felt as if she were riding a rocket, slowing only slightly to circle the barrels. Each bounce made her entire body ache, but it was worth it.

When she flew across the finish line, the crowd was on their feet cheering, and she knew she'd turned in one of her best times. Instead of looking to see the time, she moved Copper into position for her next run.

One by one, the others took their turns. Felicia, currently in first place, went after the other five and Tessa watched her make a flawless run, but Tessa knew she could beat her time.

She took off. Raced inside. Her speed was not that of her earlier run, but Copper was still flying. She relished the wind in her face. The sound of the crowd. Her horse's hooves pounding below her. And before she knew it, her last ever barrel racing run was over and so was her career.

Tessa's time flashed on the screen, and Braden shot to his feet, as did her family. She'd done it. She'd won another championship, and he couldn't wait to congratulate her. He started for the exit, but so did each and every one of the McKades— the big, boisterous family he wanted to become a part of. But to make that happen he needed time with Tessa. Time alone. So far, he'd only been able to kiss her good-night and tell her he loved her again, but after the family celebrated her rescue and Lankford's arrest, she'd been too tired for more.

And this morning, Braden had had to talk to Walt to let him know his intentions toward his daughter and to secure that job he'd offered. Then the whole family pitched in to set up the corral for a barrel racing clinic Tessa had scheduled for right after the rodeo closed. Before he knew it, it was time for the barrel racing competition, and he hadn't wanted to distract Tessa by talking about their future, so he'd simply wished her well. Kissed her on the cheek while the family watched, and left the barn to sit in the stands with them.

Now he trailed them out of the arena as Tessa dismounted from Copper, a wide smile on her face. Braden couldn't take his eyes from her. She stood tall and proud by Copper, patting his neck and talking to him. Love poured from her eyes. Love that he'd seen directed his way, too, and he could hardly stand back and let her family rush in first. But he did.

He watched, seeing Tessa looking past them all. Looking for him. Their eyes met. Longing filled her gaze, but she had no time for him right now. She had to go back inside for the closing ceremonies, then hightail it back to the ranch for the clinic.

Braden smiled at her, and when she issued him an apologetic look, he waved it off. He hoped to spend the rest of his life with her, so he could wait for now.

"This has been a perfect morning," Betty said. "I couldn't be any happier for Tessa."

Winnie looked up. "And it's great weather for the clinic, too."

"Exactly how long does this clinic run?" Braden asked.

Jed met his gaze. "We'll be done by supper time."

"Supper time!" Braden shook his head. "That won't do. Won't do at all."

The sun shone brightly over the Trails End corral. The thunderstorms had broken the heat wave, and it was a glorious day to be outdoors. The only thing that would have made it better for Tessa was if she was alone with Braden and not conducting the clinic. She'd hoped to talk to him before now, but the closing ceremonies had gone long, and she'd had to race back to the ranch, where the girls were already waiting for her.

"I'm ready," the first girl to make a run called out from atop her horse.

"Go!" Tessa pressed the button on her stopwatch to time six-year-old Kellie as she wound her horse through the clover pattern. Tessa held a Little Britches Rodeo Association clinic every year, but this was the first time she wished she wasn't there. She had Braden to thank for that. Being alone with him was all she could think about.

Kellie flashed over the finish line, and Tessa clicked the button.

Kellie trotted her horse over to Tessa. "How'd I do?"

"Three seconds better than the last run."

"Aw, only three seconds." Her lower lip came out.

"Three seconds is a big improvement," Lexie said as she came up to lead Kellie out of the ring so the next child could take her turn.

Tessa smiled her thanks to Lexie and took a quick look around the ring. She was so blessed that her entire family had turned out for today's riding clinic as usual. Kendall handled the paperwork. Lexie was the event coordinator. Mom and Nana prepared all the food and refreshments. Granddad helped with loading, unloading and grooming the horses. Her dad and her brothers took on the setup and Braden had even helped. But now he was missing in action.

Kendall had said he'd mentioned that he needed to go for a ride, but not why. He'd told Tessa twice that he loved her now, but he'd never said that he was ready for a relationship. Maybe he was thinking about that on his ride.

"What in the world?" she heard Kendall exclaim.

Tessa turned to find her sister staring across the field, her hand over her eyes to keep the sun out. A horse and rider galloped toward the corral.

She couldn't make out the rider at that distance, but she knew the horse.

Shadow. Braden's Shadow.

Kendall clutched Tessa's arm. "Do you know what he's up to?"

Tessa shook her head, as she was too stunned to see him barreling straight for them to get a word out. He soon reached the corral, and though it had been only thirty minutes since she'd last seen him, she drank in the sight of him and couldn't move. He wore jeans and a green button-down shirt that molded to his wide shoulders and had his hat pulled low so she couldn't see his eyes clearly, even though she desperately wanted to.

"Sorry if I'm interrupting," he called out.

Tessa couldn't think of what to say.

Her father came up next to Tessa and shouted, "We were just about to take a snack break."

"We were?" Tessa finally got out.

"No," her dad whispered. "But you don't want to do this with the whole family and all these kids hanging nearby, do you?"

Tessa shook her head and watched Braden slide from his horse with a swift and sure movement. He started for the fence, his cowboy swagger confident. She felt as if someone had hijacked her brain, and she couldn't think straight. She heard her family rounding up the children and heading toward the house to wash up.

Braden climbed the fence and slipped to the ground. He paused for a moment to meet her gaze, and her heart somersaulted. He crossed the space and came to a stop in front of her. He tipped his hat up, and she saw a wash of uncertainty mixed with determination in his expression.

"Hi," he said.

"Hi," she responded. "What's going on? Why are you—"

He pressed his finger against her lips to silence her. "I'm here for you."

"Me?" she squeaked out.

"When I saw you in the river yesterday, I've never been so scared in my entire life. I knew right then that I want you in my life. Every day. Every hour. I've already arranged things with your dad for a job. I respect him. All of your family. It will be an honor to work in his department."

"You talked to Dad?"

"Of course I did." He took her hands and held them. "I needed to know I'd be living here before I could talk about this with you."

"But you're a homicide detective," she said. "You don't want to go back to patrol. You might hate it, and then you'll resent me. That's no way to start a relationship."

"Your dad said one of the detectives is going to retire soon, and with my experience, I stand a good chance at getting the job." He locked eyes with her. "I love you, Tessa. Please say you'll marry me. I know this is sudden, but we'll have a long engagement if you want. Just say yes and make me the happiest guy on earth."

Before she could respond, his lips quickly claimed hers, and she couldn't move. The warmth, his touch, his nearness felt heady, and she suddenly didn't want to step even an inch away from him. Now or ever. She twined her arms around his neck. He drew her closer and deepened the kiss.

At some point, she became aware of a man clearing his throat nearby. She pulled free to see her father smiling at them.

"I take it she said yes," her dad said.

"Not yet, sir," Braden replied but didn't take his eyes from her. "If you don't need anything from us, I plan to continue convincing her."

Her father laughed deep and rumbly. "Just thought I'd mention that all eyes are pinned on you. So you might want to do that convincing elsewhere."

Braden tossed back his head and laughed. The sound was music to Tessa's ears.

"What do you say we do as directed?" he asked.

"Um, actually, I don't need any more convincing. I say yes!"

Braden scooped her up in his arms and spun her around.

"She said yes," her father yelled.

Applause broke out from her family and shouts of "Welcome to the family, Braden" followed.

"Did my whole family know?" she asked him.

"I only talked to your dad. You know, to get his permission. How many people he told, I have no idea. But I gotta think with how everyone in your family is up in everyone else's business that some of them knew."

She leaned back to look into his eyes. "And you're okay with joining a family like that?"

"Okay with it, are you kidding?" He smiled, his eyes crinkling with joy. "I can't wait to become a member of the messy, wonderful McKade family."

* * * * *

If you enjoyed this story, don't miss the exciting first installment in Susan Sleeman's
McKADE LAW *miniseries:*

HOLIDAY SECRETS

Find more great reads at
www.LoveInspired.com

Dear Reader,

I miss the days when many generations of a family often lived in the same community. There was such a sense of belonging and togetherness. A sense of working for each other's good and just experiencing pure joy in being together. I grew up in such a situation, and even though I was the family member who moved far away, I am still richly blessed from growing up in that togetherness. Maybe you had such an experience, too, or are fortunate enough to be part of a multigenerational family in one community.

In *Rodeo Standoff*, Braden has never experienced the concept of a well-knit family unit, and Tessa takes her family for granted. It's through each other's eyes that they come to see how amazing the McKades are, and I hope you saw this, too. I have loved creating and developing this family and look forward to writing the final two books for your enjoyment.

If you'd like to learn more about the McKade Law miniseries or my other books, please stop by my website at susansleeman.com. I also love hearing from readers, so please contact me via email, susan@susansleeman.com, on my Facebook page, Facebook.com/SusanSleemanBooks, or write to me c/o Love Inspired, HarperCollins, 24th floor, 195 Broadway, New York, NY 10007.

Susan Sleeman

Get 4 FREE REWARDS!

We'll send you 2 FREE Books plus 2 FREE Mystery Gifts.

Love Inspired® books feature contemporary inspirational romances with Christian characters facing the challenges of life and love.

FREE Value Over **$20**

YES! Please send me 2 FREE Love Inspired® Romance novels and my 2 FREE mystery gifts (gifts are worth about $10 retail). After receiving them, if I don't wish to receive any more books, I can return the shipping statement marked "cancel." If I don't cancel, I will receive 6 brand-new novels every month and be billed just $5.24 for the regular-print edition or $5.74 each for the larger-print edition in the U.S., or $5.74 each for the regular-print edition or $6.24 each for the larger-print edition in Canada. That's a savings of at least 13% off the cover price. It's quite a bargain! Shipping and handling is just 50¢ per book in the U.S. and 75¢ per book in Canada*. I understand that accepting the 2 free books and gifts places me under no obligation to buy anything. I can always return a shipment and cancel at any time. The free books and gifts are mine to keep no matter what I decide.

Choose one: ☐ **Love Inspired® Romance Regular-Print** (105/305 IDN GMY4) ☐ **Love Inspired® Romance Larger-Print** (122/322 IDN GMY4)

Name (please print)

Address   Apt. #

City   State/Province   Zip/Postal Code

Mail to the Reader Service:
IN U.S.A.: P.O. Box 1341, Buffalo, NY 14240-8531
IN CANADA: P.O. Box 603, Fort Erie, Ontario L2A 5X3

Want to try two free books from another series! Call 1-800-873-8635 or visit www.ReaderService.com.

Get 4 **FREE REWARDS!**

We'll send you 2 FREE Books <u>plus</u> 2 FREE Mystery Gifts.

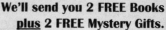

Harlequin® Heartwarming™ Larger-Print books feature traditional values of home, family, community and most of all—love.

FREE Value Over **$20**